# PONY CLUB SECRETS

# ✣Issie✣
## and the
# Christmas Pony

# The Pony Club Secrets series:

## Also available:

# PONY CLUB SECRETS

## Issie
and the
# Christmas Pony

# Stacy Gregg

HarperCollins *Children's Books*

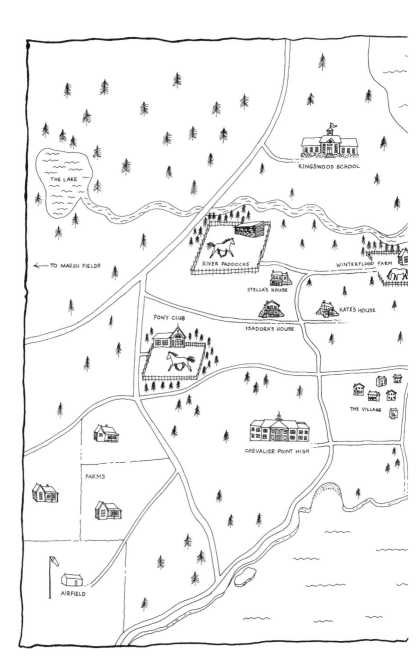

# For Hayley and all the kids in Room 10, Merry Christmas

# www.stacygregg.co.uk

First published in Great Britain by HarperCollins *Children's Books* in 2008.
HarperCollins *Children's Books* is a division of HarperCollins*Publishers* Ltd,
1 London Bridge Street, London SE1 9GH
This edition published in 2015

www.harpercollins.co.uk

ISBN-13 978-0-00-728874-8

Printed and bound in England by Clays Ltd, St Ives plc

Find out more about HarperCollins and the environment at
**www.harpercollins.co.uk/green**

# CHAPTER 1
## *A Summer Christmas*

Issie Brown was just a little girl when she realised that Christmas was all wrong. Not wrong exactly, but sort of mixed up, muddled. *Not the way it should be.*

Christmas on TV was always cold and wintry. There were sleigh bells and snow and you crowded round a roaring fire with hot chocolate while your mum cooked roast dinner with turkey and plum pudding. You'd wrap up warm in coats and mittens to sing carols and then tuck yourself up indoors and watch the snowflakes patter against the window while you waited for Santa to arrive.

Issie couldn't make head nor tail of it. Because Christmas wasn't like that at all in Chevalier Point. It wasn't snowing for starters – in fact, it was positively baking hot, the middle of summer, without a cloud in the bright blue sky. And there wasn't any turkey or plum pudding. Issie couldn't remember ever eating that sort of food for Christmas. For as long as she could remember her family had cooked their Christmas lunch on the barbecue down at the beach. They would wake up on Christmas morning and open their presents, which nearly always included a beach toy like swingball or a boogie board. Then they'd race down to the beach, where Issie would meet up with Stella and Kate.

While their dads put crayfish and scallops on the hotplate to sizzle and their mums set out the picnic blankets, the girls would swim in the sea, riding the waves in on their boogie boards. When lunch was ready, they'd sit down on the blankets, still wearing their swimming costumes, letting the hot sun dry their backs as they ate. Their plates would be piled with bright red crayfish claws, which they would smash open with nutcrackers, prising out the juicy white flesh, dipping it in hot melted butter and mopping up the juice with crusty bread.

For dessert there would be pavlova and strawberries and ice cream, and afterwards Issie,

Stella and Kate would lie back on the grass in the hot summer sun until their mums were convinced their food had been digested and it was safe to swim again.

No roaring fire, no snowflakes. It was a very different Christmas. A New Zealand Christmas.

It was hard to believe that when it was summer here in Chevalier Point, on the other side of the world it was winter. Right now, it was midnight in Europe and all the kids were fast asleep. Here, it was midday on Christmas Eve. The weather, as usual, was gloriously sunny, and Issie was in the kitchen at her house with Stella and Kate. The girls had come up with the genius idea of making Christmas cakes – with their own very special recipe.

"I need more oats!" Stella was using a wooden spoon to stir the mixture in the mixing bowl. It was already so thick that the spoon actually stood straight up in the bowl even when she wasn't holding it.

"Here!" came a voice from underneath the bench. Kate, who had been rummaging around below the sink, popped her head up and passed the bag of oats to Stella.

"I've got the apples too," said Kate. "I'll start chopping."

"I've found the secret ingredients!" Issie came

through the door carrying a bag of something that looked like lawn clippings and a plastic bottle filled with thick black syrup.

"Perfect!" Stella said. "You put it in the bowl while I stir."

As Issie sprinkled handfuls of alfalfa on top of the mixture, Stella's vigorous stirring sent bits flying everywhere.

"Hey, I think it still needs more oats," Kate said, grabbing a handful out of the bag. "Oops!" She had managed to miss the bowl and drop the oats on the floor.

"Kate!" Stella shrieked. "You're getting it on my shoes!" There were oats all over the floor and alfalfa bits stuck to the walls.

"Ohmygod..." Issie giggled. "If mum sees this mess, she'll..."

"She'll what?" The girls turned round to find Mrs Brown standing in the doorway behind them. She did not look best pleased that her kitchen had been turned into a bomb site.

"What on earth is going on in here? What are you girls doing?"

"Hi, Mum!" Issie grinned. "I know it's a bit of a disaster, but we'll clean it up."

"Yeah, Mrs B," Stella chimed in. "We were going to tidy up when we finished."

"Finished what?" asked Mrs Brown. "Isadora? What are you up to?"

"We're making Christmas cakes!" replied Issie brightly.

Mrs Brown looked at the suspicious line-up of ingredients on the bench. "With molasses and chaff?" She wrinkled up her nose. "Issie, why didn't you ask me to help you girls? I've got a great Christmas cake recipe…"

Issie laughed. "No, Mum. Not for us. Christmas cakes for the ponies!"

"We're going to make them in these." Stella pointed to a stack of old plastic ice-cream tubs on the bench beside her. "That way each horse gets their own cake."

"And we'll use slices of carrots and apples to decorate the tops," added Kate.

Mrs Brown shook her head in disbelief. "Do you think your ponies actually know that it's Christmas tomorrow?"

"Toby knows," Kate grinned. "He's got a list of things he wants from Santa."

"What's on the list?" asked Stella.

"A new summer rug, some floating boots, one of those cool pink riding crops…"

"I hardly think Toby would want a riding crop!" Issie giggled.

"Yeah, good point," mused Kate. "I didn't think of that when I was writing the list!"

"I've asked for a new bridle," Stella said, "and some proper long black leather boots. But the ones I want are really expensive. Mum said if I'm lucky, Santa will get me some black rubber ones at least."

"What about you, Issie?" Kate said.

"What?"

"What do you want for Christmas?"

"I really want some new jods," Issie said. "Mine are all too small."

"All your clothes are too small," said Mrs Brown. "When you turned fourteen you shot up like a beanpole." She smiled at her daughter. "I think Santa can probably stretch to a pair of jodhpurs. In fact, there's a suspiciously jodhpur-shaped present under the tree with your name on it."

Even though it was just Issie and her mum at home for Christmas, there were loads of gifts under the tree. Issie's Aunty Hess had sent her a present, wrapped in the most wonderful pink and gold horsey paper. (Issie was pretty sure it was a new halter for Storm.) There were a couple of gifts under there from her dad too – mailed at the last minute as usual. Issie had given one of the boxes a shake and it sounded like a board game of some sort. He usually sent her a board game. The other gift was about the right size and shape to be a Barbie doll. Issie had learnt by now not to be disappointed by her dad's presents. Last year he gave her a book all about fairies with glitter on the cover that was totally babyish. It was like he didn't realise that she was fourteen now, and still treated her like a kid. In his mind, Issie was still the same nine-year-old she had been when he had left. She hardly ever saw her father. He had remarried and had a new family – Issie had a half-sister and a half-brother – so he never came home to see her at Christmas time.

Issie missed her dad at Christmas. Even if his presents did, well, kind of suck. It seemed strange without him here, with just Issie and her mum.

"Is one of those presents under there for me?" Stella asked hopefully, eyeing up the tree.

Issie pointed at a small package wrapped in pink and red candystripe paper. "That little pink one at the front is for you from me, and the purple one is for Kate."

"Ohhh… let's see!" Stella rushed over to the tree and prodded her package. She let out a shriek. "Is it a dandy brush?"

Issie looked crestfallen. "Stella, you're not meant to guess! It's supposed to be a surprise." She watched Kate holding up her present, which was really badly wrapped and quite obviously shaped like a sweat scraper, the curved rubber sort you use to dry off a wet pony.

"I think I can guess what mine is too," Kate grinned.

Mrs Brown shook her head at them. "I can't imagine what we used to buy you lot for Christmas before you had ponies. Your Christmas lists read like a tack-shop inventory."

"I can," Stella said. "I mean, I can remember what it was like before we had the ponies." She looked at Issie. "Do you remember that Christmas when we went on the pony-club camp? You know, the Christmas you got Mystic?"

Issie felt a shiver run through her as Stella said Mystic's name. Of course she remembered that Christmas. She remembered that it was their first ever Christmas without her dad, which had been awful. But in a way, it also turned out to be the best Christmas she had ever had. It had been the start of everything.

When Issie looked back on that time now, she realised that Mystic was meant to be hers – that their lives were inextricably intertwined somehow. Of course, back then she couldn't possibly have known what was to come. That Mystic would be taken away from her so tragically. And how could she possibly have known that his death was not the end at all, but the beginning? Issie's bond with the little grey pony was so deep and so powerful that her horse would never really be gone. Whenever she needed him most he was there to watch over her and her horses and keep them safe. Not like a ghost or anything, but as a real horse, flesh and blood. Right by her side for the rest of her life.

At Christmas time, more than at any other time, Issie found herself recalling memories of the times before Mystic died, when he was still with her as a regular pony. But most of all she remembered the Christmas when she and Mystic first met. Had she found Mystic or had he found her? It didn't really matter. What mattered most was that, with each day, she realised more and more just how magical that Christmas had been.

"I remember," Issie said to Stella. "I remember…"

# CHAPTER 2
### *...Four years earlier*

Issie stared into the eyes of the giant pink pig. Gently she reached her hand under its belly. Her fingers fumbled around, grasping the cork. With one swift tug she released the stopper and a waterfall of money cascaded noisily out of the pig's tummy on to her duvet. She pushed the ten and twenty cent pieces to one side and began picking out the notes and the gold $1 and $2 coins.

"Isadora? Are you dressed yet? You need to leave in ten minutes!" Mrs Brown called up the stairs.

"I'm just finishing something!" Issie yelled back. She was already in her uniform and her hair was brushed. All she needed to do was pull on her school shoes and she was ready. But first she wanted to check how much she had in the piggy bank. She sat cross-legged among the coins on her bed and began to sort the money, counting in her head as she went.

"Do you want a banana in your lunchbox?" her mum called up the stairs.

"Mum! You made me lose track!" Issie sighed and put all the ten cent pieces back into the pile to start again.

"What?" her mother shouted back.

"Nothing!" said Issie distractedly. She carried on counting. "That makes $5 dollars, plus another $5 is $10..." Issie had been saving up for a pony ever since she could remember – from the moment her mum told her that if she was really serious about getting a pony then she would have to buy one herself.

"If I save up enough to buy one then can I really have one?" Issie had asked.

"Well... yes, I suppose so," Mrs Brown had agreed.

"How much is enough?"

"I should think about $1000 would be enough to buy a pony," her mum had said.

Years later, Mrs Brown admitted that she never thought Issie would reach $1000. "I didn't think you were serious," Mrs Brown recalled. "I thought it wouldn't take long before you gave up on the whole horse nonsense and splurged it all on toys instead."

But Issie didn't give up. She saved and saved – all her birthday money and pocket money from doing chores. It took ages for the pig to fill up, but eventually the coins were crammed past its tummy all the way to the snout and the pig was so heavy Issie could hardly lift it.

There was the moment of triumph when she finally reached her goal of $1000 – followed by bitter disappointment when her mum still refused to buy her a pony. "You're only nine years old; that's too young," Mrs Brown had said. "A pony is a big responsibility, Issie. You have to be able to groom it and feed it and take care of it. They're a huge commitment."

"I know that!" Issie had insisted. "I will look after it. You said I could have one when I had $1000."

But Mrs Brown was firm. "Wait until you're ten. Ten is a good age for a pony."

Wait until she was ten? This, as far as Issie was concerned, was changing the rules halfway through. In fact, Issie would have pointed out exactly how unfair this was, but she figured that since she was already nine and three-quarters – which was so close to ten anyway – she would take the new deal that was being offered.

It wasn't that much longer to wait. And her mum couldn't wriggle out of it this time. Once Issie turned ten she had to let her have a pony. Didn't she?

Issie's tenth birthday arrived in September. Mrs Brown came up with a new excuse. "It's practically still winter," she reasoned. "There's no point in buying you a horse when it's too wet and cold to ride."

Issie had protested that she didn't care about the weather, but her mother had stood firm. And so Issie waited. She watched the seasons change and the days get longer. It was December now, summer was here and she was ten years old *and three months*. Her piggy bank was now bulging with a whopping $1274 – thanks in part to two rather large birthday cheques from both her grandmothers. This time when she approached her mother, she was bound to win the fight. Mrs Brown was completely out of excuses.

Issie bounded down the stairs from the bedroom into the kitchen and put the piggy bank down on the table with an emphatic thud. Mrs Brown looked up from her newspaper. She saw the familiar face of the pink pig and sighed. "How much is in there now then?"

"$1274," Issie said as she pushed the pig closer to her mother. "Please?" she begged as she nudged the piggy bank across the table until it bumped into Mrs Brown's coffee cup. "Mum, please! You said I could get a pony when I was ten and I was ten ages ago…"

Mrs Brown looked back at the paper as if she were hardly listening, "Did I say that? That you could have a pony when you were ten?"

Issie's face dropped. This couldn't be happening! "Mum! Don't you remember? You said when I was ten! We talked about it!"

Mrs Brown gave a heavy sigh. She had been wishing and hoping that it wouldn't come to this. Hoping that this whole pony thing was just a phase. But here she was, being confronted by a ten-year-old with a pink pig full of cash. She looked up from the newspaper and saw the desperate look on her daughter's face, her trembling lower lip as she fought to hold back the tears. At that moment Mrs Brown knew that she had lost the battle and her daughter, finally, had won.

"All right," she said. "I was just winding you up. I did say you could have a pony when you were ten, didn't I? And I can see I'm going to be forced to keep my promise."

"What?"

Mrs Brown smiled. "We'll look at the horses for sale in the paper when you get home from school, OK? And we'll go online and look at that horse trader website. What's it called again?"

"Trade-a-pony!" Issie's voice was trembling. She had waited for her mother to say this for so long now, had pestered and begged her every day, but it never seemed as if this moment would ever arrive. And now, here they were. It was finally happening!

"Mum?" Issie asked. "Do you really mean it?"

Mrs Brown nodded. "I think it's time to buy you a pony."

Issie squealed with delight and threw her arms around her mum's neck, giving her the biggest hug ever. When she had stopped hugging her mum, she began to pogo about the kitchen, jumping up and down with excitement. "Can we look for a pony now? Please? I can go get the paper!"

"You seem to have conveniently forgotten the little matter of going to school!" Mrs Brown laughed. She picked up Issie's schoolbag off the chair and stuffed a lunchbox in it along with a drink bottle and a book bag before passing it to her daughter. "There'll be plenty of time for horse-hunting when you get home.

Why don't we find a few ponies worth looking at and we can go out and see them this weekend?"

"Thanks, Mum!" Issie's voice was a high-pitched squeak. "I don't believe it. I'm really getting a pony!"

"Go on!" said Mrs Brown. "Canter off or you'll be late for school."

Stella almost burst with excitement when Issie told her the news. "Ohmygod, Issie! This is so cool!" she squealed. "I bet you get your new horse in time for pony-club camp!"

"Shhh!" Issie muttered at Stella. Their teacher, Miss Willis, was giving them a stern look. They were supposed to be doing silent reading with their library books – not talking about ponies.

As far as Issie was concerned, there were only two kinds of kids at Chevalier Point Primary School. There were the ones who were totally horse-mad (like her, Stella and Kate) and then there was the rest of them. Issie couldn't understand how anyone could not like horses. Especially when you lived in a place like Chevalier Point. The town was horse heaven, surrounded by rolling green fields, perfect for grazing your pony. The pony club was within hacking distance and there were beaches and forests to ride in.

At lunchtimes at school the "horsey girls" all got together to play horsey games – cantering back and forth over skipping ropes, finding acorns and pretending they were mixing them up for hard feed for their imaginary horses.

Issie, Stella and Kate had always been friends, but this was the first year that they were all in the same class. Their teacher, Miss Willis, was widely considered to be one of the nicest teachers in the whole school, but even Miss Willis sometimes lost her patience with the whole horsey business. All the girls ever wanted to do was write stories about horses or draw horse pictures for their art projects. The three of them had been warned loads of times that they would be made to sit at separate desks if Miss Willis caught them chatting about ponies again when they were supposed to be working.

Looking up at their teacher now to check that she wasn't watching them, Kate lowered her voice to a whisper. "It might take you ages to find a pony!" she said. "We looked at loads before we finally bought

Toby. It took months! There's no way you'll have a pony in time for camp."

Issie's smile evaporated. Kate was always so sensible, which could be really annoying sometimes. But she was right. It could take ages to find the perfect pony.

"Mum says we're going to start looking this weekend so you never know. It's only the first of December – that gives us a whole month," Issie said, trying not to sound deflated.

"You'll find one straightaway!" Stella said breezily. "And then we can all go to pony camp together!"

The Chevalier Point Pony Club camp was coming up in the first week of the Christmas holidays and it was all Stella and Kate could talk about. They were going on a trek for three days, carrying their lunch in their backpacks and having picnics by streams. They would ride all day and then set up camp at night. Their parents would meet them at the camp grounds with their sleeping bags and stuff so that they didn't have to carry it all on their horses.

Stella and Kate had both joined the Chevalier Point Pony Club earlier in the term. They both had their own horses, a fact that made Issie insanely jealous, even though her friends tried not to rub it in.

"You can't be jealous of Coco!" Stella would giggle. "She's a total hand-me-down!" Coco used to belong to Stella's big sister Penny, but Penny had lost interest in riding lately. "All she cares about is her stupid boyfriend!" scoffed Stella. And so Stella had been given Coco. The thirteen-two chocolate brown mare could be a bit lazy sometimes, but she was great at games and jumping and Stella loved her to pieces.

It hadn't been so bad when it was just Stella who had her own horse, but then last month Kate got Toby, a big bay Thoroughbred, and now all the two girls ever talked about was pony club, and how much fun it was. Issie felt left out. It wasn't Stella and Kate's fault. They were really nice about it. They let Issie have rides on Coco and Toby and help groom them and stuff. But it wasn't the same as having her own pony.

Issie was desperate to go to the camp. But she knew Kate was right. The chances of finding a pony to buy in time were pretty slim. Issie's Aunty Hess, who had just bought her own horse farm and knew loads about ponies, had told her that good learner's ponies were as scarce as hen's teeth. Issie wasn't quite sure what she meant by that, but apparently it had something to do with being hard to find.

"Maybe you'll get a pony for Christmas!" Stella whispered far too loudly. She had never really mastered the whole whispering thing.

"Yeah," said Kate. "It'll be gift-wrapped under the tree with a big bow tied around its tummy!"

Stella glared at Kate. "It might happen!" she insisted. "You never know. Like Issie said, she might find the perfect pony this weekend."

"I hope so," Issie said. "How cool would that be?"

"Muummm, I'm home!" Issie came into the kitchen to find her mother at the table with a cup of tea and the paper.

"Look at this!" Mrs Brown said, passing Issie the newspaper which was folded over neatly to the Horse and Ponies for Sale section. She must have already been through the ads because one of them was circled in blue pen. The ad was headed up in bold black type:

**For sale – genuine learner's pony**

*14 hh grey gelding. Six years old.*
*Loves to jump and has no vices. Sadly*
*for sale as owner overcommitted. A*
*great pony for a beginner.*
*$1000. Hurry!*
*At this price he will be sold quickly!*

Issie read the ad back to herself twice. "What does 'no vices' mean?" she asked.

"I asked your aunt about that," said Mrs Brown. "It means they don't do anything naughty like buck or kick or bite."

Issie nodded. She looked back at the ad again. Fourteen hands was quite a big pony, but Issie was tall for a ten-year-old. And a grey? She didn't want to jinx it by telling her mum that grey was her absolutely favourite horse colour right now.

"Mum!" Issie was so excited the newspaper was trembling in her hand. "He sounds perfect!"

"He does, doesn't he?" Mrs Brown smiled. "Hen's teeth? My foot! It looks like we just found you a pony."

# CHAPTER 3
*The Perfect Pony?*

It took ages for the weekend to come. Well, actually, it took the same amount of time that it always did, but it felt like forever to Issie.

After they saw the ad for the pony in the paper her mum had phoned up and made an appointment to go and see him on Saturday morning, and ever since then Issie had spent the week feeling sick with excitement.

In the car that morning, Issie had to resist the urge to ask if they were there yet. Her mum hated it when she did that. Instead, she sat in the passenger seat positively twitching with expectation and, just when she didn't think she could stand it any more, her mum said, "Ah! Here we are!" and turned the car down a narrow gravel driveway.

Issie could see a paddock ahead of them. There was a corrugated iron shed with a hitching rail next to it and a little grey pony tied up with his saddle and bridle already on. Issie's heart skipped a beat as she realised that this must be him. Her new pony.

Mrs Brown parked the car and turned to Issie. "Well, what do you think?"

Issie wasn't sure what to say. She realised now that she had been expecting it to be love at first sight. But the pony didn't look at all the way he had sounded in the advertisement. He was really skinny and bony. Issie could actually see his ribs sticking out. His head was hanging down in a miserable kind of way and, despite being saddled up, he hadn't been brushed and his coarse, dull coat was covered with caked-on mud.

"Well," said Mrs Brown uncertainly, "he's not in very good nick, is he? He needs a good brushing for a start. Still, he looks very sweet, don't you think?"

Actually, Issie thought the pony didn't look the least bit sweet. He looked sulky and mean. His dark eyes glowered at her and his ears were permanently pinned flat back against his head – which Issie recognised as a sure sign that a pony is angry or upset.

Issie's mum didn't seem to notice these things.

She knew nothing about ponies. Mrs Brown didn't even like horses. It was Issie's Aunty Hess who was the horsey one in the family. The only problem was, Hester was so busy getting the stables ready for her new horse-training business, she didn't have time to come and help Issie buy a pony.

When Mrs Brown had phoned her sister last night to get some advice on how to go about buying a horse, Hester was adamant. "First of all," she said, "I don't think you should be buying one at all, Amanda. You know nothing about horses!"

"I'm sure I can manage," Mrs Brown had replied huffily.

"Not without a professional there to help you," Hester insisted. "It's a tricky business buying horses. A dishonest business too."

"But, Hess, the pony in the paper sounds lovely!" Mrs Brown had argued.

"They all sound lovely, Amanda!" Hester had snapped. "But I think you'll find that those ads in the paper very rarely have much to do with the truth of the matter."

"Well," sighed Mrs Brown, "can't you at least give me some pointers so that I'm not completely green when I go in there and look at these horses." There was silence on the other end of the phone.

"All right," Hester said reluctantly. "I'll tell you some of the really obvious stuff to look out for. But please, Amanda. Promise me you won't buy Issie a pony without having it properly checked by someone who knows what they're doing. If you wait a month or so, I can come and help you, but right now I can't leave the farm…"

"And Issie needs to get a pony by Christmas or she won't be able to go to this camp. So just tell me what I need to know," Mrs Brown said firmly. "I'm sure I can manage."

Luckily, Mrs Brown couldn't see Hester on the other end of the telephone rolling her eyes at this.

"All right," Hester said. "There are a few basics. My first tip is that you must catch the pony yourself and saddle it up yourself."

"Why?"

Hester had boggled at her sister's lack of common sense. "For heaven's sake, Amanda! How else will you know whether he's hard to catch? A dodgy owner will catch it for you so you don't realise that the pony is difficult or naughty."

This didn't seem like such a big deal to Mrs Brown, but Hester assured her that it was. "Trust me. You don't want to buy a pony only to spend all your time chasing it around the paddock for hours – it doesn't leave much time for actual riding."

Mrs Brown had listened to her sister's advice and asked the man over the phone to leave the pony in the paddock for them to catch when they arrived. But he clearly hadn't listened as the pony was all ready and waiting, tethered to the rail and saddled up.

"Not a good start," Mrs Brown said ominously as she got out of the car. She eyed up the pony. "He does look skinny, doesn't he?"

Issie got out of the car too and began to walk over towards the grey pony. She was still a few metres away when the pony began to back away nervously, jerking his head against the lead rope.

"Hey, boy," Issie said softly under her breath. "What's your name, huh?" She stood still and waited for the pony to calm down, talking to him the whole time. Slowly, very slowly, Issie stepped forward and reached out to stroke the pony's mud-caked coat. The little grey flinched as Issie tried to pat him and then he started to back away again.

"It's OK, boy." Issie spoke softly to the pony. "I won't hurt you…" The pony didn't understand Issie's words, but he did seem to grasp her meaning. He stopped trembling so much and stood still as she ran a hand down his neck.

"Good boy, easy now," she murmured to him. "There's nothing to be frightened of…"

As Issie said this, the grey pony's mood changed. He flattened his ears back against his head and pulled against the lead rope. He looked totally terrified as he strained against the railing, trying to free himself.

"What's wrong, boy?" Issie couldn't figure out what had the pony so spooked. Then she heard a noise behind her and turned to see a blue truck pulling up and a man in a pair of grey overalls coming towards them.

"Easy, boy," Issie tried to calm the pony. "It's just a truck." But surely the pony already knew that? It looked like the truck driver was his owner, so why was the pony so scared?

"You must be Amanda." The man in the overalls stuck out his hand to Issie's mother. "I'm Paul," he said. "I see you've already met Apache."

Paul stepped towards the pony, and Apache

instantly put his ears flat back and shook his head violently up and down, making it quite clear that he wasn't interested in making friends. *Stay away from me!* he seemed to be saying.

The man growled at the little grey and raised his hand as if he was going to hit Apache, terrifying the pony even more; the whites of his eyes showed with fear as he strained against the rope, trying to get away from the man.

"Leave him alone. You're scaring him!" said Issie.

"Just teaching him who's in charge," the man replied gruffly. He went to raise his hand again then saw the look of horror on Issie's face and thought better of it. He dropped his hand and changed his tone, his voice suddenly oily with charm. "Good lad!" he said to the grey pony. "You're a lovely pony, aren't you? Shall we show this young lady what a good pony you are?"

He turned to Issie and spoke to her in the same way, his words positively dripping with fake sincerity. "Is he going to be your pony, sweetheart?" Issie nodded mutely. "Well, you'd better get on and have a ride then," the man said. "Apache will be fine once you get him going. He just hasn't been ridden for a while."

"Wait a minute," said Mrs Brown anxiously. "How long since he's been ridden?"

The man shrugged nonchalantly. "It's been a few months I guess. But he's dead quiet. The perfect learner's pony, like I said in the ad."

Mrs Brown didn't look convinced. It didn't help that Apache was still straining at his lead rope and dancing about nervously. His ears stayed flat back and he was swishing his tail. He most certainly did not look like a learner's pony. Mrs Brown shook her head. "This horse looks half wild to me. And my daughter is not getting on him," she said firmly.

"No, Mum," Issie said. "Honestly, it's OK. I'll try him."

Mrs Brown was about to object, but Paul was too quick for her. "That's the spirit!" he said, promptly unhitching the grey pony and leading him out into the paddock.

"Issie..." Mrs Brown began.

"I'll be fine, Mum," Issie said. "Please? Let me try him?"

Paul already had Apache ready and waiting. "Here," he said to Issie. "I'll give you a leg up."

Apache danced about nervously on the spot and Paul struggled to hold the grey pony still so Issie could mount. Despite what she had said to her mum, Issie was dead nervous. She wasn't at all sure that she wanted to go through with this. Apache had looked so sad and so skinny before, but now that she was about to get on him he looked totally panicked. Could she ride this horse? There was only one way to find out.

Issie tightened the strap on her hard hat and took a deep breath as she felt Paul's hand wrap around her knee, legging her up into the saddle. She barely had the chance to sit down and hadn't even managed to get her feet in the stirrups when Apache started bucking.

Although the grey pony was nothing but skin and bone, he still had enough energy to instinctively try and throw anyone who got on his back. As soon as he felt the weight of a rider in the saddle Apache did three swift little pig-jumps. The first of these unseated Issie, the second threw her forward so that she was hanging on to his neck and the third buck dislodged her entirely. She flew through the air and hit the earth with a bone-crunching thud that left her lying winded and stunned on the ground.

"Issie!" Mrs Brown rushed forward.

Issie managed to get to her knees, but she was struggling and heaving to get her breath back. She held her stomach and took in great gulps of air. The fall happened so quickly that she found herself crying from the shock, hot tears running down her cheeks. She brushed them away roughly with her sleeve.

"Are you OK?" Mrs Brown bent to hug her.

"I'm fine, Mum, honest," Issie said, pushing her mum away and standing up. She looked over at Apache who seemed quite relieved to have dislodged his rider so quickly and was now trotting away happily to the other side of the paddock out of his owner's reach.

Mrs Brown turned to Paul. "What are you playing at?" she said furiously. "Putting a child on a horse like that? Apache is hardly even broken in!"

Paul objected to this. "He's just a bit fresh, that's all. I've never seen him do that before. He's got a heart of gold…"

"You should be ashamed of yourself," Mrs Brown fumed. "Trying to sell that beast to a child as a learner's pony!" She turned to Issie. "Get in the car," she said. "We're leaving."

Mrs Brown ranted non-stop the whole drive home. "You could have been killed!" she fumed. "That pony was dangerous – I should never have let you get on him. Learner's pony? More like a bucking bronco!"

"It wasn't Apache's fault!" Issie tried to stick up for the grey pony. "He was just scared."

"I'm sure he was!" said Mrs Brown. "That big oaf is obviously very brutal to the poor animal. Your aunt was right," she continued. "It's a dishonest business buying and selling horses. That man was a total liar. I doubt that horse was even broken in. And did you see the state it was in? I've got a good mind to report him to the police."

"Can we do that? Tell the police on him?" Issie asked. "Maybe they'd help Apache…"

Mrs Brown shook her head. "Honestly, Issie, I would call the police in a heartbeat, but I really don't think they want to know about dodgy horse dealers. He's not actually committing a crime, is he?"

"But he was really cruel and awful!" Issie insisted. She felt herself getting tearful again, but they were tears of anger this time. "We can't leave poor Apache with him."

"No," Mrs Brown agreed, "we can't. And I don't

intend to either." She pulled the car up in the driveway of their house and strode inside. She went straight to the phone in the hallway and began to leaf quickly through the phone book.

"Who are you calling?" Issie asked.

"I don't know. There must be a listing for a horse protection society or something in here. There must be someone who deals with people like that. They need to see how malnourished and mistreated that poor pony is." She flicked through the book and found what she was looking for.

"Ah – here it is – The International League for the Protection of Horses. There's a number here for the local ILPH branch." Mrs Brown dialled the number and held the phone to her ear. "It's ringing," she said to Issie. "Quick! Run into the kitchen and get me a pen and paper." Issie raced off and by the time she was back her mum was finishing up the conversation.

"Terrific," she said. "Thank you so much. No, that's great. We can come to you straightaway. If you give me your address, we'll be there in five minutes..." She gestured to Issie to hand her the pen and then frantically scribbled something down.

Mrs Brown hung up the phone. "Well, that was

the man from the horse protection league. He was very helpful. Turns out he doesn't live far from here; he moved to Chevalier Point just a few months ago. I got his details – we can go round there now, fill in the paperwork and file a complaint." She passed Issie the piece of paper she had just scrawled on. "Hang on to this for me. It's the address. I'll just grab my coat."

Issie looked at the bit of paper in her hand, deciphering the familiar messy, looped letters of her mother's handwriting. She had written the street address first: *127 Esplanade Drive.* And there, beneath the address, were the words that would change Issie's life forever: *Tom Avery at Winterflood Farm.*

# CHAPTER 4
## *Winterflood Farm*

On the way to Winterflood Farm, Mrs Brown started to have second thoughts.

"Sweetie," she said, "I think we have to face reality. I can't buy you a pony. I have absolutely no idea what I'm doing. I don't even know what half the words in the ads mean. Look at what just happened! That pony sounded perfect to me and he was a total nightmare!"

Issie felt a chill run through her as she saw her chances of ever getting a pony slipping away. "You mean I'm not getting a pony after all?"

"I didn't say that," her mum corrected her, "but it's certainly clear to me now that we can't do it alone. We need help."

"Stella could come and look with us," Issie suggested.

Mrs Brown didn't look impressed. "I was thinking of someone a little more experienced and mature than Stella." She sighed. "If only Hess wasn't so busy with the new farm." She looked at Issie. "I'm afraid we may have to put these pony plans of yours on the back burner again and wait until your aunt has time to help us."

"But, Mum!" Issie couldn't believe it. "It's nearly the Christmas holidays. I'll miss pony camp! It's not fair!"

"Isadora!" her mother snapped. "You could have been killed today on that half-wild horse. I'm not racing out and buying you a pony until we have some expert advice and that's final. I don't want to hear another word about it!"

Mrs Brown's mood didn't improve when they arrived at 127 Esplanade Drive and no one answered the front door. "I don't get it," she groaned as she hammered for a third time on the door of the small cottage. "He knew we were coming. I only phoned up ten minutes ago. Where has he gone?"

Issie looked at the Range Rover and horse truck parked in the driveway. "His car is here so he can't have gone out. Maybe he's round the back of the house and he can't hear us," she suggested. "I'll go and look." The gravel driveway made a crunching sound under Issie's boots as she walked round the side of the cottage, past the horse truck and the dark green Range Rover, and through a rose arbour that led to the rear of the cream stucco cottage.

"Hello?" she called. "Mr Avery?" There was no reply. Issie walked down the path a little further. Ahead of her, directly behind the cottage, were five paddocks, all of them neatly fenced by elegant, dark-stained wooden fencing. Running round the perimeter of the farm was a well-trimmed dark green hedge, just like the one that lined the driveway at the front of the house. It all looked very equestrian, Issie thought, like something out of a magazine. There were even a couple of showjumps set up in one of the paddocks.

In the paddock closest to the house, two horses grazed beneath the shade of a sprawling magnolia tree. One of the horses, a big chestnut with a white star on his forehead and two white socks, stopped grazing and raised her head to look at Issie.

*Imagine…* Issie thought as she stared back. *Imagine having horses grazing just outside your back window, right next to the house.* Issie's house had a fair-sized back garden, but her mum had planted it with lots of flowers which, as far as Issie was concerned, were just taking up valuable pony space. Issie had gone through the garden one day with a measuring tape and had figured out that if you pulled up all the flowerbeds and put down more grass, you would almost have room to graze a horse. But her mum, for some reason, didn't agree with this plan.

There was still no sign of Mr Avery. Issie headed back in the other direction, past the rose arbour where she had come in and down the path between another row of hedging where she could see a small block of stables ahead of her. The stables were dark-stained wood, just like the fences. There was a sheltered washing bay for hosing down the horses at the entrance, and then a row of three neat loose boxes, all freshly mucked out with clean straw on the floor, their green double doors hanging open.

"Mr Avery?" Issie called out. At the end of the stables there was another door which looked like it might lead somewhere. Issie tried the handle and the door swung open to reveal a rather scruffy but professional-looking tack room. There were stacks of hay and sacks of horse feed, and saddles and bridles hanging from racks. On the desk at the end of the room was a computer surrounded by piles of paperwork. But what really caught Issie's attention was the wall above the desk, which was festooned with satin ribbons, the sort that you win at horse shows. There were loads of them, all strung up together so that they arched in a shining rainbow across the wall with their fancy gold and silver tassels dangling down at each end.

Issie read the curly writing on the ribbons: things like *1st place Team Area Trials Championship* and *Eventer of the Year.* Hanging on the wall directly beneath the ribbons were framed photos of lots of different horses – chestnuts, bays and greys – but the rider was always the same. He was lean and lanky, with a handsome face and masses of unruly brown curls sticking out from under his riding helmet.

There was one really old and faded photo of him where he looked almost as young as Issie, smiling for the camera and proudly holding up a wooden trophy covered in little gold shields. In the other photos he looked much older, and he was jumping over really enormous cross-country fences. Issie's favourite was a framed print of the man riding a chestnut horse and jumping over a giant flower pot. She put out a hand to touch the picture when a man's voice behind her startled her and made her jump back.

"You like that one? It's my favourite too," she heard him say. "It was taken at the Badminton Horse Trials. Starlight was spooked by the flowers. I had to kick her on to get over it, but she was fine after that and gave me a lovely clear round."

Issie turned around to see a man leaning in the doorway behind her. He looked familiar somehow and then she realised why. His face was the same one she had just been looking at in all the pictures. He looked a bit older than in the photographs, but he still had the same curly brown hair which was now trying to escape from beneath a cheesecutter cap. He wore a navy jumper, dark tan riding breeches and a pair of green Hunter wellingtons.

"That's you in the photo?" Issie asked.

"The last time I looked it was," the man said with a grin. "That chestnut jumping the flowerpot is Starlight. She was a brilliant mare in her day, but she's retired now. You probably saw her as you came in here – she's grazing in the magnolia-tree paddock."

Issie remembered the horse with the two white socks. It was the same horse in the picture! "You mean you've ridden at the Badminton Horse Trials?" Issie couldn't believe it.

"Quite a few times actually..." the man said, gazing at the photos, "but I'm like Starlight I suppose. I retired from that sort of thing a while ago."

"You don't look that old!" said Issie.

The man laughed. "Thanks!"

"I'm sorry," Issie stammered. "I meant you don't look old enough to retire."

"Ah well," the man said. "There's a story there. You see, I took a bit of a tumble on the course at Badminton. I was on my favourite horse. His name was The Soothsayer. We were at the Vicarage Vee and he slipped coming into the fence..." He trailed off and didn't finish the sentence. "Anyway, that was a long time ago. I'm guessing you're not here to talk about my former riding career. You must be the girl that phoned up about the mistreated horse?"

"Yes... well, no... well, kind of. It was my mum who called you. We thought maybe you could help us?"

The man looked at her kindly. "I'm sure I can. That's what I'm here for..." He paused. "I'm sorry. I don't think you told me your name."

Issie grinned. "I'm Isadora Brown. But my friends call me Issie."

"Nice to meet you, Issie." The curly haired man stuck out his hand for her to shake. "I'm Tom Avery."

# CHAPTER 5
## *Bombproof Bert*

It turned out that as well as being a champion rider, Tom Avery made a very good homemade chocolate slice. He served up a plate of it with afternoon tea, and Issie gratefully munched down three big pieces while Mrs Brown filled in all the official ILPH paperwork and Avery explained what would happen to Apache.

"Now that you've made a complaint, I'll visit the horse myself and see what condition the animal is in – to establish whether he's really been mistreated. After what you've told me, I think it's highly likely this horse will get signed over into our care. We have a strong case here to remove him from the current owner and relocate him. We'll take him to an ILPH farm, get him healthy again and they'll reschool him and find him a new home."

"Will he be OK?" asked Issie. "He looked so miserable. He was really skinny and covered in mud..."

Avery nodded. "You'd be amazed at the recovery that some of these horses can make. But it takes time..."

"Is there any chance he'd be OK in time for pony-club camp – it's in three weeks!" Issie blurted out the words and then instantly regretted it. She sounded so selfish!

Mrs Brown explained. "Isadora really wanted to go to pony camp and we were trying to buy a pony before the Christmas holidays so she'd be able to ride with her friends..."

Avery shook his head. "Well, you certainly won't be going to pony camp on Apache. From what you've told me, that horse will need quite a while to recover. He'll have to be properly fed and retrained. It could take as much as two or three months to get him back in shape. Even then, I doubt he'd be a suitable mount for a young rider like yourself who's just starting out."

Issie tried not to look too disappointed, but inside she could feel her heart breaking. She knew that

Apache wasn't the right horse for her, but she wanted a pony so desperately.

"Are you looking at any other ponies?" Avery asked Mrs Brown.

Mrs Brown sighed. "Apache was the first one and he was a total disaster! I was just saying to Isadora on the way here that we might have to give up on the whole pony business – for a while at least." She stood up to leave. "Anyway, we shouldn't take up any more of your day. Thank you for all your help and for the tea, Tom."

"Yes, thanks," Issie said. "I'm so glad you're going to help Apache."

Avery looked at the crestfallen expression on Issie's face. "Listen," he said, "do you have a bit of time before you go. While you're here, I think you should meet Bert."

Bert turned out to be a stocky strawberry roan with a hogged mane and a short cropped tail that he swished back and forth vigorously whenever he moved.

"I was out the back in the arena behind the stables with Bert when you arrived," Avery explained. "Bert's an ILPH rescue horse. I've been reschooling him for the past few months here and he's just about to go to a new home."

"He's beautiful," Issie whispered as she stepped forward to pat Bert's velvety muzzle.

"Bert's not the best name in the world – but then I didn't come up with it," said Avery.

"I think Bert is a lovely name." Issie felt that she had to stick up for the pony.

"He's a good-hearted sort, aren't you, Bert?" Avery gave the pony a pat, then he turned to Issie. "So how about it? Do you want a ride?"

Issie felt her heart skip a beat. "Really? Would that be OK?"

"Absolutely," Avery said. "That is, if it's OK with your mother." He looked at Mrs Brown.

"Please, Mum!" Issie pleaded.

"Is he safe?" Mrs Brown asked. "After that other horse today I'm really not sure…"

"Bert is bombproof," said Avery.

Mrs Brown looked terrified at this. "Who on earth would let off a bomb next to a horse?"

Avery grinned. "Bombproof just means that a horse is unfazed by anything and is excellent to handle under any conditions. Just like Bert here."

"Ohh!" said Mrs Brown.

"You don't know anything about horses, do you?"

"Not a thing," Issie's mum admitted. "Just my luck to end up with a horse-mad daughter."

"Well, Amanda," Avery smiled at Mrs Brown, "you'll have to trust me. I would never put your daughter in any danger. She'll be fine on Bombproof Bert."

After the disaster with Apache that morning, Issie was totally expecting her mother to say no. So she got quite a shock when Mrs Brown looked Avery in the eye as if she was about to make a very serious decision, paused and then finally nodded and said, "All right."

"Thanks, Mum!" Issie couldn't believe it.

"On you hop then," said Mrs Brown. "Quickly, before I come to my senses!"

"Come on," said Avery. "Let's take him into the loose box and I'll show you how to get him tacked up. Then we'll find a helmet to fit you and we can get started."

Once Bert was tacked up, Avery gave Issie a leg up on to his back and led her through to a small, bark-covered outdoor arena at the rear of the stable block.

"Have you ever had a riding lesson before?" he asked. Issie felt a bit embarrassed to admit that she hadn't. She had never done anything much more than walk on a horse before and now she was being taught to ride by someone who'd got a clear round at Badminton!

"Don't be nervous," Avery said. "We'll just do the basics today, OK?"

He spent the first couple of minutes adjusting Issie's stirrups, showing her how to sit in the saddle, how to hold the reins so that the leathers ran through between her bottom two fingers and up again, pinned underneath her thumbs.

"Your heels must stay down," Avery said. "Put all your weight into them." He adjusted her grip on the reins. "And your hands must stay still and not jerk the horse in the mouth. Now look where you want him to go. You're going to ride him forward towards those trees over there. Just give him a squeeze with your legs, not a kick, and ask him to walk on. OK? That's it! Excellent! Well done!"

Issie tried her hardest to concentrate and listen to every word Avery was saying. It wasn't easy. Sometimes he would tell her to keep her heels down and her hands steady and her back straight and her eyes up and she felt like her brain was going to burst thinking of so many things at once. But Avery spoke calmly and quietly to her and never lost his temper when she got something wrong. And Bert was such a good horse. When Issie asked him to trot by giving him a gentle tap wih her ankles, the pony sprang instantly into a steady stride, bouncing her around in the saddle.

"That's it!" Avery called out. "When his trot throws you up out of the saddle like that, just go with the movement and rise up in the stirrups with the beat. When I call out I want you to rise… and up… and up… and up…"

Issie couldn't believe it! She was posting! She had learnt how to do a rising trot just like that!

"Are you ready to try a canter?" Avery called out to her as Bert circled at a trot. Issie felt her tummy fill with butterflies. A canter? Even Stella and Kate were only just learning to canter! Issie swallowed her nerves. If there was one thing she knew about horses, it was that they could tell if you were nervous. She tried to stay calm and focus on her instructor's advice.

"You're going to put your inside leg forward at the girth and your outside leg back," Avery said.

"Then you'll pick up your reins a little and sit heavy and ask him to canter. OK? Are you ready? Canter!"

Bert struck off immediately into a canter and Issie couldn't believe it. All her life she had loved ponies to pieces. She loved to touch them and brush them and care for them. She felt connected to them. But now that she knew what it was like to actually ride one – to canter on a horse – it was beyond anything she had felt before. It made Issie feel complete somehow, as if she had finally found the one thing in her life that she wanted to do for ever and ever. Cantering on a horse had to be the best feeling in the whole world!

"And steady down, Bert…" Avery's voice was deep and slow as he spoke to the pony, asking him to slow his stride. Bert instantly responded, going from a canter to a trot and back to a walk. "Good boy… good Bert. And halt! That's a good boy!"

Avery walked out to the edge of the arena and took the roan pony by the reins. "How was that?" he smiled up at Issie. It was at that moment that Issie realised she was just sitting there with a big dumb grin on her face that wouldn't go away.

"I loved it," she said. "Thank you." She patted the roan pony. "Bert is so cool!"

Avery looked intently at Issie. "Was that really your first time on a horse?"

Issie nodded. "Well, Stella and Kate – they're my best friends – they've let me sit on their horses and led me around and stuff. But I've never actually ridden one by myself before."

Avery seemed surprised. "You've got a great seat. You're a natural rider. I've never seen anyone learn as quickly as you did today."

"Really?" Issie was thrilled.

"Here," Avery said, "let me show you how to dismount properly and then you can put Bert away for me. I need to talk to your mum."

Years later, Issie would still wonder what Avery had said to her mother that day. Was it really the way she rode Bert that made him decide to help her? Or was it the fact that Issie and her mum so obviously knew nothing about horses and he could see that they needed him? Issie liked to think that it was because Avery could see into her heart and knew that she loved horses, really loved them, just like he did when he was her age. Whatever it was, by the time she came back from the stable, it had been decided.

"Tom is going to be giving you riding lessons," Mrs Brown told her excitedly. "I thought I'd buy you a daily lesson for the next fortnight – you can have it as an early Christmas present." Issie was thrilled.

"I don't usually take on novice pupils," Avery added, "but you're not like any novice I've seen before, Issie. You've got enormous potential. And Bert is the perfect mount for you to learn the basics."

There was more news though. "Issie," Avery said, "I've been talking to your mum about buying you a pony and she asked me whether I could sell you Bert." Issie's heart stuck in her throat. "You rode Bert very well," said Avery, "but unfortunately he isn't mine to sell. Bert's an ILPH pony and we've already found a guardian for him. I can give you some lessons on him over the next couple of weeks, but after that he's going to his new home."

Issie was bitterly disappointed at this news but tried not to show it as Avery continued. "I explained to your mum that finding a good learner's pony is almost impossible..." He saw Issie's crestfallen expression. "...almost impossible – but it can be done. And if you'll let me, well, I'd be happy to help."

Issie was stunned. "You mean it?"

"I do." Avery smiled at her. "The perfect pony is out there somewhere, Issie," he said. "And together, you and I are going to find him."

# CHAPTER 6
### *Dream Pony*

True to his word, Tom Avery started hunting for a pony for Issie. But, just as he said, the search wasn't proving to be an easy one. He and Issie had been poring over the Horses for Sale ads in the paper and on the internet, but days had gone by and they still hadn't actually been to look at a single horse.

Horse-hunting with Avery was almost as bad as it was with her mum, Issie realised. At least Mrs Brown thought every single horse in the paper sounded marvellous. Avery went to the other extreme. He would vet the ads so thoroughly that it never even got to the stage where Issie had the chance to try the horse out. There was always something wrong with the horses. Avery wasn't foxed by the cunning way the ads were phrased and would pick up on the truth behind the words instinctively.

"What about this one?" Issie would say hopefully. "Novice eventer, five years old, has been turned out and is just coming back into work, needs confident rider…"

Avery would shake his head. "Needs a confident rider? You can translate that to mean he's a total handful! The fact that the horse has been left unworked probably means he was badly behaved and his former owner lost their nerve. They're too scared to get back on him."

"OK, well, this one sounds brilliant!" Issie moved on to the next ad. "Wonderful first pony-club mount. Would suit learner rider…"

"Yes," Avery couldn't help smiling, "but you didn't read the next line where it says he's only ten hands high!"

It was always the same: either the horses weren't quite right – too big, too small, too inexperienced, too many problems – or the ones that were all right were simply too pricey and cost an absolute fortune.

"Eye-catching first pony, three lovely elevated paces…" Issie began to read the ad. "Oops, oh no! Forget it – that one is $12,000!" Suddenly, Issie's budget of $1000 looked impossible.

"It's not much money, is it?" Issie sighed. "I mean, I've actually got $1274, but I need some money to buy a saddle and stuff as well, so really I guess $1000 is the most I can spend."

"It's not impossible to find a pony for that price," said Avery. "It's just a bit harder, that's all." He suggested they look for ponies who were a bit older. "You can find a good learner's pony who is as old as eighteen or twenty. My first pony Queenie was twenty-two years old and she was lovely. And we might be able to get one at a price you can afford – older ponies are cheaper."

Issie wished she could be as positive as Avery. She didn't want to admit it because he was trying so hard to help her and everything, but she was beginning to despair. It was only another two weeks until school finished, and then it would be Christmas holidays and the pony camp.

"Don't worry," Avery insisted. "I'm sure something will turn up soon."

But how? None of the ads in the paper seemed quite right. Avery had made a few phone calls, but he wasn't satisfied that any of the ponies he'd enquired about were suitable and Issie still hadn't even tried out a single horse.

Wednesday's paper held a bit more promise though. In the middle of the horse section was an ad boxed out with huge bold type: **HORSE AUCTION.** Underneath the headline the ad read:

### HORSE AUCTION

*Over fifty horses and ponies for sale.*
*All breeds and sizes. Sport horses and*
*pleasure hacks. Auction Saturday 20th,*
*Mackenzie's Farm, Lone Pine Road.*

"That's the weekend before Christmas! I could have a pony in time for camp!" Issie couldn't contain her excitement. But Avery looked less certain.

"We'll definitely go along and check it out," he told her. "I've had a few fantastic bargains in my time at the auction yards. But buying horses that way can be risky. Often the only horses that come up for sale at auction are the ones that aren't good for anything except the knacker's yard."

"What do you mean? What's a knacker's yard?"

Avery looked serious. "There are some horses that even the ILPH can't save, Issie. They're either very old or they've been so mistreated by bad owners that they've turned wild and uncontrollable. Those horses usually end up being sold at auctions, which is why dealers from the knacker's yards go along to bid, hoping to pick up a cheap deal."

"What happens to horses at the knacker's yard," asked Issie uncertainly, not convinced she wanted to know the answer.

"Well, sometimes they get used for things like – like pet food," replied Avery gravely.

"That's horrible!" Issie said. "Can't the ILPH stop it?"

"Not really. These are horses no one else wants," Avery said. "And honestly, Issie, they're treated very humanely. Anyway, most of the yards have closed down now. Hardly anyone makes pet food like that any more."

Still, Issie felt so sick at the thought, she couldn't bring herself to feed the cat that evening when she got home. She looked at the side of the pet-food can. "Mum? Do you know what sort of pet food we feed Mitzy?"

"What do you mean?" asked Mrs Brown.

"Well…" Issie didn't know how else to explain it. "Do you think it has ponies in it?"

"Let me take a look…" Mrs Brown began to read the fine print on the tin. It turned out that the pet food didn't contain any ponies, which was lucky for Mitzy who was very keen on dinner and couldn't see what the hold-up was all about.

That night, before Issie went to bed, she picked up the piggy bank and held it in her hands, trying to gauge how much money was in there by its weight in her hands. She had added another $15 in the past week – pocket money for doing chores. There must be almost $1300 by now. Enough to buy a pony at the auction maybe. After all, it wasn't like Issie was expecting to get a fancy show pony with papers or anything. All she wanted was a pony that she could ride to pony club and groom and care for. A pony that would be her best friend in the world. It wasn't too much to ask, was it? *Yeah, right,* Issie thought. *In your dreams. In your dreams…*

The grey road snaked through the fields. On either side were tall trees, their spindly trunks reaching up like bleached bones towards the sky, casting long black shadows in the evening light.

*This is creepy. I want to turn back*, Issie thought.

But then came a stronger emotion, from somewhere deep inside her. *No turning back. You must keep going. You have to find him.*

The fields surrounding the road seemed grey and watery, like a photograph with all the colour drained out of it. Up ahead, the red barn was the one bit of brightness on the horizon. It stood about twenty metres back from the road, accessed through a metal gate. The gate was shut and beyond it Issie could see well-worn tyre tracks that led past an old rusty tractor, with ragwort and hemlock sprouting up between its wheels, all the way to the open barn doors.

*This is the place,* Issie realised. She could feel her heart thumping in her chest as she climbed over the gate and began to walk towards the barn. The sound of her heart beating in her ears made it hard to pick out the hoofbeats at first. Then she heard the unmistakable nicker of a horse calling out and there he was, trotting round the side of the barn to greet her.

In the fading light it was hard to make him out at first, but as he came closer Issie could see that he was a dapple-grey pony, not much more than fourteen hands high. He had coal-black eyes which shone with a quiet intelligence as he came towards Issie with his head held high. His mane, which was thick and long, was swept back by the wind and his thick, silvery tail trailed behind him. His dapples had faded a bit with old age so that his coat was now snowy white in some places, with dappled patches on the rump and withers. Although his back was swayed from age, he still had good conformation, stocky and compact, and he moved with such grace. Issie thought he was the most beautiful horse she had ever seen.

The pony kept trotting towards Issie, his stride high and bouncy. Then, when he was just a few metres away, he halted. He looked at Issie, and for a moment the girl and the horse connected, and Issie knew right then and there that she had found him.

*You're the one*, she thought. *You're mine.*

But the grey pony seemed uncertain. He pawed the ground with his front hoof, flicking his head up and down as if he was trying to make his mind up about something. Then he wheeled about on his hocks and cantered off, back round the side of the red barn and out of sight.

"Wait!" Issie called after him. "Don't leave!" She desperately wanted to stop the pony, to make him stay with her, but she didn't know what to do.

"Don't go..." Issie murmured. "Don't leave... Come back. Please, don't leave me! How will I find you?"

Then came the sound of her name, a voice calling to her. "Issie? Issie!" Hands softly shaking her awake. Her mother's arms wrapped round her. "Issie? Are you OK?" And suddenly she was no longer in the field next to the red barn. She was in her bed and her mum was there too, snuggling her tight, whispering to her that it would all be OK, that it had just been a bad dream.

"I'm all right, Mum," Issie managed. "I'm sorry I woke you up."

Mrs Brown looked worried. "Dreaming about your dad again?"

Ever since her father had left, Issie had been having bad dreams. She would wake up sometimes in tears, not remembering the details of her dream and not knowing why she was crying. Her mum had become used to the nightly ritual of coming into her daughter's room to settle her down again with reassurances. Tonight, as far as Mrs Brown knew, was the same as any other night. Except it wasn't.

"No," said Issie, "I wasn't dreaming about Dad this time, Mum. It was about my horse."

"Sweetie," Mrs Brown said gently, "you don't have a horse."

Issie felt confused. It was hard to believe she had been dreaming – the grey pony had seemed so real, as if she could have reached out and touched him.

"But there was a grey horse…" Issie trailed off. Had it really just been a dream?

Mrs Brown tucked the blankets in tightly and kissed her daughter on the forehead. "Go back to sleep, OK?"

"OK, Mum."

Issie didn't sleep. She lay in bed and stared at the ceiling, her mind racing. She didn't care what her mum said. She knew it sounded crazy, but it had been more than just a dream. The grey horse and Issie were connected somehow; she could feel it. "He's real," Issie told herself. "He's real and he's mine. All I have to do is find him."

# CHAPTER 7
## *The Chevalier Point Pony Club*

Issie's horse-hunt was going nowhere fast – but at least her daily lessons with Tom Avery and Bert were going well.

"I've never had a student who focused so hard or improved as quickly," Avery told her, making her glow inside with pride.

Avery had been giving Issie lessons every day after school in the arena at Winterflood Farm. He was an exacting instructor and would drill Issie as if they were in the army. He was the sergeant-major in the centre of the ring, barking instructions to her as she rode around, concentrating hard on trying to do just as he said.

On the very first day Avery made Issie ride without stirrups to improve her balance. Issie was terrified at first, but it worked. When she took her stirrup irons back again she found that her position was greatly improved and she was much more secure in the saddle.

"You should take your stirrups away for five minutes or so at the start of every lesson," Avery told her. "You'll be amazed at how good it is for developing an independent seat."

On the second day Avery gave Issie a short, round wooden stick which she had to hold in both hands as she rode, bridging across the mane so that she would learn how to keep her hands even and steady when she held the reins.

On day three Avery turned up with a book tucked under his arm. "What's that for?" Issie asked nervously.

"Oh, this?" said Avery casually. "I want you to ride around the arena with it balanced on top of your helmet to make sure that you're keeping your eyes up and straight ahead."

Issie boggled at this. "Really?"

Avery grinned. "No! Of course not. I'm just joking." He held up the book so that she could see the cover. "This is my old pony-club manual," he said. "It's essential reading for riders who are ready to sit their first club certificate." He passed the book to her. "I thought you might like to have it."

Issie didn't know what to say. Finally, she managed an embarrassed "thank you" and took the book.

"So," Avery said briskly, "you can take it home with you. You won't have time to read it now. Today we're practising our transitions from walk to trot and we're going to learn how to change the rein in trot!"

Issie loved Avery's lessons, but they always left her utterly exhausted. "You're quite fit," Avery would say, "but riding uses different muscles to any other sport, and you have to become horse-fit."

He was right, Issie realised. When she got off the horse at the end of the lesson her legs and arms would ache from using muscles that she never knew she had. Avery would make her do the same things over and over again until she got it right, and after a couple of weeks of Avery's tuition, Issie realised she had actually become quite confident in the saddle – and in the stable. Avery insisted that Issie learn how to do all the grooming and tacking up as well, so that she was quite capable of looking after Bert all by herself, as if he were her own pony.

The only problem was, Bert wasn't hers. He

belonged to the ILPH which meant that one day soon he would have to go to the new guardians who had been chosen to care for him.

"Next week!" Issie was shocked when she arrived at Winterflood Farm one day after school for her regular ride and Avery broke the news. "But that's so soon!"

"Issie," Avery reasoned, "you always knew this was going to happen."

Issie sighed. "I know, I know, it's just that Bert and I were just starting to click – you said so yourself!"

Avery looked thoughtful. "I can't change the fact that Bert is leaving," he said, "but how would you like to do something really special with him before he goes?"

"Like what?"

"I thought you might want to take him to pony club. There's a rally this Sunday," said Avery.

Issie was stunned. "Really? But that's only a couple of days away. Do you think I'm ready?"

Avery nodded. "Absolutely. I was planning to go along myself anyway. Chevalier Point's head instructor has just left the club so I'm going to be taking over as of this season." Avery had been keeping very quiet about this development so this was all news to Issie.

"My best friends Stella and Kate both go to that club!" she said excitedly.

"Excellent!" Avery said. "Well, no doubt I'll be meeting them this Sunday." He smiled at Issie. "So, how about it? Are you keen to come along? Bert floats well, so it would be no trouble to load him into the truck. You'll need to become a club member of course – I've got the paperwork around here somewhere; we can fill it in. The club uniform is a navy knitted jersey and a red tie with a white shirt, but since this is your first time, they won't expect you to be in uniform. Just wear something tidy with your best jods."

Issie couldn't believe it. Her first club rally.

"Excellent!" Avery said. "That's settled then. Be here at 6 a.m. on Sunday morning and we'll head off."

"Why do these horse things have to be so early?" Mrs Brown stifled a yawn. It wasn't even light outside yet and they were driving towards Winterflood Farm to get Bert ready for the rally day. "6 a.m.!" Mrs Brown groaned. "Even the birds aren't up yet!"

Ever since Issie had started her lessons at Winterflood

Farm, her mum had been driving her back and forth each day after school to ride. Mrs Brown said she didn't mind, but Issie wished she had a bike. It was only a ten-minute trip to Winterflood Farm, and if she had her own bike she'd be able to go and visit Avery and the horses any time she liked.

"It could be worse," Issie said cheerily. "At least Bert has a hogged mane so we don't have to be there at 5.30 a.m. to plait up!"

"What a bonus!" groaned Mrs Brown.

In fact, Avery had Bert all groomed and ready in his floating rug and boots by the time Issie and her mum arrived. He lowered the ramp of the horse truck and gave Bert's lead rope to Issie. "You can lead him on if you like," he said. "Turn him round to face the truck and then walk him up; he'll follow you." Issie felt nervous, but Bert stepped obediently behind her up the ramp and tethered quietly in the horse truck next to his hay net. "Issie can ride with me in the truck if she likes," Avery told Mrs Brown. "We'll see you there!"

The pony club was only about ten minutes drive away. Issie felt sick the whole way. She had been excited by the idea of her first club rally, but now she felt nervous, really nervous.

"Something up?" Avery noticed how quiet she was.

Issie didn't know how to say it, but finally she blurted it out, "All the other riders are going to be better than me."

Avery nodded. "That seems quite likely since you've only just started riding," he said. "You can't expect to be the best rider at the club on your first day."

Issie sighed. "You're really not making me feel any better here. Shouldn't you be telling me how good I am?"

"Issie," said Avery gently, "I've ridden at the Badminton Horse Trials against some of the best riders in the world. Don't you think I felt the same way when I turned up there for the first time? I worried that I was out of my league, that all the other riders were better than me. That fear never goes away, no matter how experienced you are. But it shouldn't stop you. I went to Badminton because I knew that I wanted to ride with the best, to learn everything there was to know about horses. It's not about being on top – it's about the journey that takes you there."

He smiled at her. "We all have to start somewhere Issie. You have the talent and the natural ability to be a great rider. Right now, you're still a beginner, but one day that will change. This is the first step. Your first time at pony club." He pulled the truck up at the gates of the club grounds and looked at Issie. "Are you ready?" he asked seriously. "Because it all begins right here. This is where you start to become a real rider."

Issie nodded. "I'm ready."

"Excellent," said Avery, grinning. "Hop out and open the gate, will you? I'll park the truck under those trees over there and we'll unload Bert."

Issie was just bringing Bert down the truck ramp when she heard her name being called and saw Stella riding towards her on Coco. The chocolate brown mare came trotting up, followed by Kate on Toby. Both girls pulled their horses up alongside Avery's truck and dismounted beside Issie.

"Is this Bert?" Stella said. "Oh, he looks like a total and utter sweetheart! I can't believe this is the last time you're going to ride him before he has to go away to his new home! How awful!"

Kate looked at Stella as if she was a complete

and utter twit and hissed through gritted teeth, "Stella! I'm sure Issie doesn't want to think about that! How would you feel if someone was coming to take Coco away?"

Stella shrugged. "Oh, today they can have her! She's being so naughty. When we hacked up here this morning from the River Paddock she would barely move a hoof! She was a total slug! Then when we get here and she sees the other horses, she starts jumping around like she's a racehorse in the starting gates. She's completely bonkers!"

Kate, who had given up on Stella saying anything sensible, turned her attention to Bert. "Isn't he a cool colour?" she said to Issie.

"He's a strawberry roan," said Issie authoratitively. She would never have known this if Avery hadn't explained it to her – she would probably have described Bert as pink. He was a sort of rosy chestnut colour with lots and lots of white hairs muddled all through his coat, which made him look, well... pink was probably the best word for it.

"Issie, you'd better hurry and get him tacked up," Kate said. "It's our first rally today with Mr Avery, our new head instructor, and we don't want to be late."

Stella and Kate had never met Avery. "You've been having lessons with him, haven't you?" Stella asked Issie. "What's he like? Everyone's been going on about how great he is, but he's probably just like the last instructor: a total fossil, at least a hundred years old and really, really boring…"

"Actually," Tom Avery's voice behind Stella made her turn around, "I'm thirty-six and I promise I'll try my best to be extremely interesting."

Stella winced. "Issie!" she hissed. "You should have warned me he was right there!"

Issie gave Avery a grin. "Tom, these are the friends I was telling you about. This is Kate Knight and Stella Tarrant."

"Nice to meet you, girls," said Avery. "I'm Tom Avery. Your new head instructor."

If the day got off to a dodgy start, it quickly improved. The riders all lined up for inspection at the start of the ride, and then Avery divided them up into groups, putting Stella, Issie and Kate together with two boys they had never met before.

"I'm Ben," said the first boy, introducing himself. "And this is Max."

"Hi, Ben," Issie said to the first boy. "Hi, Max." Issie smiled at the good-looking boy sitting on the grey horse next to Ben. He grinned back, his blue eyes laughing at her.

"I'm not Max!" he said. "Ben's horse is called Max!"

"Oh!" Issie said. "Sorry! I thought…"

"My name is Dan, Dan Halliday," the blond boy said, "and this is my horse Kismit." He gave the fleabitten grey gelding that he was riding a slappy pat on his glossy neck.

"Nice to meet you, Kismit," Issie said to the pony. "At least your name isn't confusing! This is Bert," she told them. Then she hastened to add, "He isn't really mine." And before she knew it, Issie found herself telling Dan and Ben the whole story, about how she had met Avery and how the instructor had given her lessons on Bert until she could buy a pony of her own.

"I hope something comes up at the auction," said Ben. "It's only a couple of weeks until pony camp."

*Twelve days actually*, Issie wanted to say. She knew exactly how far away pony camp was. Her chances of going were dwindling by the day. She guessed she had been hoping in her heart that maybe Avery would say she could keep Bert for an extra couple of weeks and ride him at the camp before he went to his new owners. But as they came to the end of the rally that day and they loaded Bert back up into the truck, she realised this simply wasn't going to happen. Stella had been right. This was the last time she would ride the little strawberry roan.

At least it had been a fantastic farewell. After all her fears about being a total beginner, Issie actually found herself loving her ride at the club. Bert was a superstar, doing everything perfectly.

They spent the morning in the arena doing basic dressage, which at pony club everyone called "flat work". Bert walked, trotted and cantered on cue as if he had been at Chevalier Point his whole life.

Despite Stella's fears, Tom didn't prove boring at all. After the flat-work training, their new head instructor set up bending poles and barrel races and had bags of lollies as prizes for everyone who made it through to the finals. Then, after lunch, it was time for jumping.

"Can everyone take their stirrups up two holes to jumping length?" Avery instructed.

"Ummm, Tom?" Issie had a worried look on her

face as her instructor walked over to see what was wrong. "I don't think Bert and I are ready to jump yet," Issie admitted. "We've never even tried it before."

Avery took a leather strap and tied it around Bert's neck. "That's a neck strap for you to hold on to in case you lose your balance," he explained. "That way, you won't jerk back over the jumps and jag Bert in the mouth. Now, all you need to do is stay forward in two-point position like I showed you at home," Avery said. "Turn him straight at the fences, stay in stride, give him a tap with your heels just before the jump and then Bert will do the rest."

And he did. There was a whole jumping course and OK, the jumps were tiny, but Issie managed to steer her horse around the course nicely so that Bert, who was a very honest jumper, did a totally clear round the first time!

After all her fears, rally day had turned out to be one of the best days Issie had ever had.

"Thanks for letting me bring Bert today," she said to Avery as they untacked him.

"I think Bert enjoyed it as much as you did," Avery replied.

"Will I see him again before he goes?" Issie asked as

she helped her instructor wrap the floating bandages round the pony's legs. She was trying not to get upset, but already she could feel the tears welling up in her eyes.

Avery shook his head. "I guess not. His new family are coming to the farm to pick him up tomorrow." He looked at Issie, who was battling bravely not to cry. "Why don't you come home to the farm in the horse truck with me and Bert now? You can give him his hard feed and let him loose in the paddock one last time."

And so Issie rode home from her first day at the Chevalier Point Pony Club, not with her heart full of joy as she had been expecting, but with a pain in her chest that felt unbearable as she realised that she and Bert were about to part for the very last time. She stood in the paddock at Winterflood Farm as the sun set and snuggled into the strawberry roan's neck, feeding him peppermints out of her pocket and trying not to cry too much. Then she sniffed back her tears and gave Bert one last hug, holding him tight as she said goodbye.

# CHAPTER 8
### *Auction Day*

Avery arrived on the morning of the auction with his horse float attached to the Range Rover. When he saw Issie's eyes light up, he shook his head. "Don't get your hopes up," he told her. "It'll probably be coming home empty. I wouldn't count on finding a horse at this auction. It will probably be full of the problem animals that their owners can't get rid of any other way." Issie knew that. And she was trying not to get her hopes up. But the harder she tried the worse it got.

Bert had been gone for a week now and Issie really missed him. Being suddenly alone again without a pony was awful. How bad would she feel if she didn't have a pony for the whole of the holidays? This was her last chance to find one before Christmas, and if she didn't, her chances of making it to pony camp were pretty much non-existent.

As the Range Rover cruised out of town and headed through the rolling farmland of Chevalier Point, Issie was one big ball of nerves. While her mum and Avery chatted away in the front seat she sat in the back feeling positively sick, overwrought with excitement.

As he turned down Lone Pine Road, Avery passed Mrs Brown the road map. "Can you look up the address for me?" he asked.

"Don't you know where it's being held?" asked Mrs Brown.

"Uh-uh. This is the first auction they've held at MacKenzie's Farm," Avery said. "I've never been here before."

Mrs Brown took the map from him and checked the address. "According to this, the farm should be about another two kilometres down the road," she said.

Issie looked out of the window ahead of her and was struck with a sudden sense of *déjà vu*. There was something so familiar about this road, the way the winding snake of grey tarmac cut through the faded hills. Issie felt a strange sense of premonition as she stared out at the bare, pale branches of the slender trees.

*Ohmygod!* she thought to herself. *I know this place!*

"Pull over up there!" she told Avery. "Ahead of us, where that red barn is, there's a gate that will lead you through to the farm."

"How do you know that?" asked Avery.

"Because," Issie said, "I've been here before."

She had been here. But when? How? Issie's heart skipped a beat. *The dream that she'd had — the grey pony!* She remembered every detail of it so vividly. When she had woken up afterwards it had been so clear in her mind, as if it had really happened. Now here they were — this was the same place she had dreamt about! Everything was as she remembered it: the road, the ghostly trees, the red barn. The only difference was the sign that had been erected by the side of the road **AUCTION TODAY** and the fact that the metal gate was open this time.

Avery drove straight through, nosing the Range Rover down the rutted dirt track towards the barn. "What do you mean you've been here before?" Mrs Brown said, turning around in her seat to look at Issie. "When did you come here?"

"Ummm... school trip... last year... you know?" Issie said. Her mother arched a quizzical eyebrow at this, but she didn't ask any more questions. Issie hadn't meant to fib to her, but she hadn't known what else to say. "I saw it in my dream" would have sounded a little too kooky. Her mum might freak if Issie told her this was the place that gave her a nightmare the other night.

As they pulled the Range Rover up in the marked parking area next to the barn, Issie stared out of the window at the spot where she had seen the grey horse appear in her dream. She was expecting him to canter round the corner of the barn at any moment and stand before her just as he had done that night. But the grey pony wasn't there and the farm, which had been so eerie in her dream, was no longer quiet and empty. There were horses everywhere, being unloaded from trailers and trucks, with people grooming and fussing over them. Issie's eyes searched frantically through the crowds. How would she find the grey pony in amongst all this lot?

"Do you see one that you like?"

"What?" Avery's question brought Issie back to reality.

"No," she said. "I was just looking… there are so many beautiful horses here!"

"Well," Avery opened the car door, "we won't be able

to bid on them if we stay sitting here all day. Let's go!"

Inside, the red barn was a maze of stalls and roped-off pens, each containing a horse ready for the auction ring. Avery looked at the horse in the first pen. It was a brown gelding, about sixteen hands high, with a number 1 stickered on its rump.

"These horses here will be the first ones up in the auction ring today," Avery said, consulting the programme he'd been handed a moment earlier. "There are 122 lots going under the hammer today. The first horse goes up for auction at 10 a.m. so that gives us a bit of time." He looked round the barn. "I'll check out the horses in here. Issie, why don't you go out the back and see what else is around? If you see anything you like, take down the pony's number and details and come back and report to me, OK?"

Avery turned to Issie's mum. "Mrs B, if you wouldn't mind going to the registration desk in the corner over there and signing up so that we can make a bid? You'll need to give them all your details and get a bidder's number. We need to meet back here again at nine o'clock with a list of ponies that we want to trial."

Issie looked at her watch. It was eight o'clock now.

"Are you all right?" Issie felt a hand on her shoulder. It was her mum. "You look a little bewildered," Mrs Brown said. "Will you be OK by yourself, or do you want to wait for me to do the registration and then I can come with you?"

"No, Mum, I'm fine, honest," Issie said. She still couldn't shake the feeling that she had been here before. In fact, she was certain of it. And that meant she wasn't just looking for any horse. She was looking for him – the grey pony. He was here somewhere; she could sense it. She had to find him before the auction began.

As her mother headed towards the registration desk, Issie hurried through the barn towards the wide, sliding back doors. As she ran, her eyes scanned the horses in the roped-off stalls. There were chestnuts and palominos, a couple of skewbalds and loads of bays and browns, but she couldn't see a grey pony anywhere. He had to be outside somewhere.

Once she got outside, she realised that finding her pony was going to be more complicated than she had initially thought. The horses and ponies weren't lined up neatly in a row for inspection; they were scattered all over the place. Some of them, mostly the young colts and yearlings, were being kept all together in the cattle pens near the barn. Others were tethered to trucks and floats or grazing in the roped-off pens that ran in strips between the horse floats. It was like a maze!

Issie began to work her way down the first aisle of trucks and floats where horses and ponies with numbers on their rumps were tethered. Issie noticed that, as well as the number on their rump, each pony had a sheet of paper pinned next to it with the pony's details written up in thick black type. She walked up to the first pony in the aisle, a pretty, creamy coloured horse with a chocolate mane and tail, and read the paper which was plastered to the horse float beside it. **LOT 72**. The description read:

**Three year old dun mare**
**12 hands high, no vices, recently broken in**
**Expected price range: $500-$1500**
**Name: Chico**

"Hello, Chico!" Issie giggled. The little pony's forelock was so long and thick that Issie couldn't even see Chico's eyes. She was pretty sure that Chico couldn't see out from beneath all that hair. The mare looked like one of those ponies in a Thelwell book. At only twelve hands high Chico came up to Issie's chest. "You're too little for me," Issie told the pony gently. "Besides, I'm looking for someone else."

Over the next hour Issie kept looking. She wound her way down the rows of horse floats and trucks, always expecting to see the grey pony. In fact she saw several grey ponies, but none of them was him. Grey ponies can look fairly alike and yet Issie knew quite definitely that none of them so far was the pony from her dream. She had a snapshot of his face clearly in her mind – his silvery forelock, his deep black eyes and thoughtful expression. She would have known him in an instant if she had seen him again.

By the time she met Avery back at the barn as they had arranged, Issie was feeling deflated. She hadn't found her dream pony.

Avery, meanwhile, had found not one horse, but two. "Well, two that have definite potential anyway," he told Issie. "One of them is a very nice bay with good, solid conformation. He's thirteen-two hands high which is a good size for you, and he's eight years old with no vices. He's being sold by the owners; the girl has outgrown him. The other one that I quite like the look of is a palomino. A very striking twelve-year-old mare with loads of pony-club experience. She's won a mountain of ribbons, she's a great jumper and she'd be perfect for you, I think. We could give them both a try now. You could ride them and see what you think, and if you like them then we can bid on both and see which one we get."

Issie should have been over the moon. The auction had turned up not just one, but two ponies that Avery thought were worth making a bid for. *But*, thought Issie, *they aren't my pony*. They couldn't be. Her pony was a grey and he must be here somewhere; the only problem was she couldn't find him.

Avery's bay was called Juniper. He had a pretty face with ears that pointed in so far when they were pricked forward that they were almost touching at the tips. "That's a sign of Arab blood; this pony has good breeding," Avery said approvingly, running his hands over the bay, checking his conformation. He picked up all of Juniper's feet and examined the hooves carefully before looking in his mouth to confirm that the pony was indeed eight years old. Then he legged Issie up on to Juniper's back and they took him over to the arena to try him out.

Juniper proved to be a very well-mannered mount. "Give him a light workout to try his paces," Avery told Issie. She put her legs on and felt Juniper rise up underneath her. "What's his trot like to ride?" Avery shouted out as she breezed past him.

Issie smiled. "It's lovely! Really bouncy, but lovely!" Despite the fact Issie was still convinced that her grey pony was here somewhere, now that she was actually on Juniper and trying him out, she couldn't help but love the bay pony just a little bit.

"Ask him to canter," said Avery. Juniper's canter was lovely too. And the pony was a keen jumper. Issie took him back and forth over the trotting poles then tried him over a small jump and Juniper leapt clear with his ears pricked forward, a perfect gentleman.

"He's brilliant, Tom!" Issie beamed from ear to ear. Maybe her obsession with the grey pony from her dream was just silly. There was nothing wrong with Juniper; he was really lovely. "I think we should definitely bid on him," she told Avery.

If Juniper was good, then Goldie the palomino proved to be even better. Issie loved the golden mare's peppy paces. Goldie's owners showed Issie all the ribbons the mare had won. There were so many, it looked like Goldie had cleaned up at every gymkhana she'd ever been to. "Plus she's good in traffic and good to float," Avery said. "A perfect pony-club mount."

"So which one shall we buy?" Mrs Brown asked Issie and Avery.

"We bid on them both and wait and see what happens," advised Avery. "Goldie is number 50, so she'll be in the auction ring first. If we miss out on her, we put in a bid on Juniper, OK?" This seemed like a good idea to Issie. With two ponies to bid on, she was bound to have one to bring home in the horse float at the end of the day.

The auction was already under way and Issie stood at the edge of the ring, watching the horses being led in for bidding to begin. The auctioneer stood on a platform to one side of the arena. He spoke very, very quickly, rattling on to the crowd as he asked them to bid more and more for the horse that was being led around in circles in the ring. "How much am I bid for this bay mare, sixteen hands? Who'll give me $200? Do I hear 200? I have 200. Who will give me 300?" he called. Only the way he said it, it was all jumbled in a blur of words:

"How-much-am-I-bid-for-this-mare? Who'll-give-me-two-hundred? Two-hundred!"

Issie watched as horse after horse went under the auctioneer's hammer. Some of them sold for thousands others for just a few hundred dollars. Lot 42, though, a brown mare, was different somehow. When she walked into the ring it was clear that the horse was very old. She had a ewe neck, a straggly mane and tail, and the bones stuck out on her rump from lack of condition.

She looked, Issie thought, like a horse that no one loved. And it turned out to be true. The auctioneer egged everyone on, but no matter what, no one would bid on her. In the end, just one man raised his hand for the mare. He was standing in a row at the back wearing a black jersey and a black hat. He tipped his finger silently to the auctioneer. "I have $50 bid!" shouted the auctioneer. "Going once, going twice... sold!" The auctioneer's gavel came down and the horse was led out of the ring, but the man in the black hat didn't even bother to go and inspect his new purchase. He stood and waited for the next lot to enter the ring so he could start bidding again. Issie stared at the man. There was something about him that gave her the creeps.

"Who is he?" she asked Avery, pointing across the ring. "Over there. That man who just bought the brown horse."

Avery looked at the man in the black jumper. "That's Nigel Christie," he said. "He runs the local knacker's yard."

Issie had known there would be horse dealers here bidding today, and yet she still wasn't prepared for the rush of emotions she felt at that moment. She was consumed with a burning anger for men like Christie. How could they do a job like that?

"Can't you stop him?" she pleaded with Avery.

Avery shook his head. "I wish I could, but Christie isn't doing anything illegal, he's just doing his job..." Issie couldn't believe what she was hearing.

"Well, I think he's horrible and I hate him," she said. Her voice was trembling as she spoke. She thought about that poor brown mare that no one loved being bought by Christie and suddenly she could feel tears coming.

"Issie, are you OK?" Avery's kind tone made it worse. Issie shook her head and then, embarrassed by her tears, she turned on her heels and left the auction ring, running towards the back door. As she ran she choked back her sobs, her breath catching in her chest as she gasped for air. Deep down, she knew Avery was right. Men like Christie were a fact of life in the horse world. But that didn't change the way she felt and it didn't stop the tears from coming. She needed to get outside for a moment, get some fresh air and calm down.

As Issie raced out of the back door of the stable she couldn't hold her sobs back any longer. Her eyes flooded with tears, which she wiped away angrily with her sleeve. Her vision was so blurred from crying that she didn't see the man coming towards her until it was almost too late.

"Hey! Watch where you're going!"

Acting on instinct, Issie leapt back and managed to get out of the way just in time as a man leading a horse trotted past, almost bowling her over.

"Sorry," she mumbled feebly.

"Are you all right?" the man asked. "I didn't even see you! You shouldn't be running around like that in the warm-up area."

"I'm sorry," Issie said again. She felt like such an idiot.

"No harm done," the man replied. He turned his attention back to the pony standing beside him.

"C'mon, boy." He picked up the lead rein and set off again at a jog with the pony trotting obediently beside him, heading towards the horse floats at the back of the barn.

Issie was so shaken, it took her a moment to pull herself together. She had nearly been knocked over and it had all happened so fast. She hadn't been able to get a good look at the man, or more than a glimpse of the grey pony he was leading. Now, though, she looked directly at the pair of them as they trotted away and she was suddenly struck with the realisation that she had seen the little grey somewhere before.

The pony was a dapple-grey gelding, with a sway back and a silvery mane and tail. It was hard to tell at first because he had his rump to her, but then, as the pony rounded the corner, he turned his head and Issie finally saw his face. It was snowy white with those wide-set, gentle, coal-black eyes. *Ohmygod!* Issie felt her pulse quicken and her heart begin to race. She couldn't believe what she was seeing. This wasn't just any grey pony, it was *the* grey pony. It was the horse from her dream.

# CHAPTER 9
### *Going Once... Going Twice...*

Issie was so stunned by the sight of the grey pony that at first she didn't react. She remained rooted to the spot, unable to move. By the time she managed to choke out a word, the man and the pony were already almost out of sight behind the horse trucks.

"Wait!" Issie cried. But the man didn't hear her and they disappeared down one of the rows of horse trucks.

Issie broke into a run, chasing after them. The maze of horse floats, trucks and makeshift horse pens was confusing, but she was pretty sure she knew where the grey pony had gone. She made a left-hand turn at the big white truck where the man and the pony had last disappeared from sight, and began to run down the aisle, looking this way and that, trying to spot them in among the other horses.

Issie was about halfway down the row of trucks and floats, and almost ready to admit that she had taken a wrong turn, when she came to a dark green, battered old horse truck parked on the left-hand side of the aisle. She couldn't see any sign of the man, but there was the little grey pony, tethered up to the side of the truck with a hay net and some water. She knew him immediately this time, and she noticed something that she hadn't seen before. There was a number stuck to his rump: **99**. He was for sale!

When he saw Issie, the grey pony raised his head and nickered to her. It was a warm, friendly whinny, as if he was trying to say, *Where have you been? I've been waiting for you!*

"Hey, boy," Issie spoke softly to the pony. Then she stepped in closer to the little grey to give him a tentative pat on his soft, velvety muzzle. The pony, however, wasn't interested in just a pat. He stepped forward too and pushed his head against Issie, trying to use her as a scratching post. He rubbed his face up and down against her T-shirt and gave grunts of satisfaction as he managed to get rid of that hard-to-reach itch on his muzzle.

Issie giggled as the pony rubbed against her so hard that she almost toppled over. "Hey!" The grey pony's sudden familiarity had taken the girl by surprise. "Hey, stop that!" Issie giggled again. "We've only just met!"

Somehow, though, it seemed like she had known this pony forever. It was as if he was already hers. But that was crazy. She didn't know anything about this pony. She didn't even know his name.

His name! If he was for sale then his name would be right there on the paperwork, wouldn't it? Issie's eyes scanned the side of the truck, looking for the auction form with all of the horse's details. She couldn't see it anywhere at first, but finally she found it plastered to the wall of the truck and hidden beneath the hay net. The ad was brief, only two lines long. It said:

**Dapple grey Gelding, 18 years old, 14 hands**
**A one-in-a-million learner's pony**

"It doesn't say his name!" Issie couldn't believe it! All the other registration papers had the horse's name on them. Why didn't this one?

"Are you interested in buying him?" The man who had nearly run Issie over moments before poked his head out of the horse truck and smiled at her. "Hey, didn't I nearly knock you over back there? I'm sorry about that."

Issie smiled back. "It's OK. It was my fault; I wasn't looking."

The man stepped down from the truck and stood next to the grey pony. "So, are you interested in him? You are looking for a pony, aren't you?"

"Yes!" said Issie immediately.

The man looked doubtful. "Buying him by yourself?" Issie could see from his expression that he thought she was just some kid bothering his pony and not a real buyer at all.

"My mum and my instructor are helping me," Issie said. "They're in the barn watching the auction."

The man perked up a little at this. "OK, well, I'm selling him on behalf of the owners," he explained. "He's not mine, so I can't tell you much about him, I'm afraid. I'm looking after half a dozen different horses for various folk today so I find it hard to keep track. All I know is what it says on the papers."

He pointed to the sheet that was half-obscured under the hay net.

"But it doesn't say anything on his papers." Issie was disappointed. "What about his name? Do you at least know what he's called?"

The man sighed. "I'm not sure. Maybe I've got it somewhere here. Let me just check..." He rummaged around on the seat of the truck, picked up a manilla folder and flipped through the contents. "Let me see..." he mumbled as he searched. "Grey pony, fourteen hands high, eighteen years old... ahhh... here it is!" He turned to Issie. "His name," the man said, "is Mystic."

The auctioneer was up to lot number 48 by the time Issie made it back to find Avery.

"Where have you been?" Avery said. "Goldie is lot number 50. She'll be in the ring at any moment."

"Tom," Issie was panting from running all the way back, "I need you to come now and look at another horse. He's the one that I want to buy!" At that moment the auctioneer's gavel came down with a loud crack and Issie and Avery both turned to look at him.

"Lot number 48 is sold for $2300!" the auctioneer shouted. "Can we have lot number 49 in the sale ring please? A piebald yearling, bred out of Majestic, by the sire Everest. Who'll give me an opening bid of $500…?"

"Issie!" Avery said, looking serious. "We don't have time to go and look at another horse now. Goldie is up in the ring after this piebald. If we don't stay here now, we'll miss our chance to bid on her."

Issie bit her lip. Avery was right. If she dragged him off now to look at the grey pony, she would miss her chance to buy the palomino.

"What lot is Juniper?" she asked.

"He's number 62," Avery said. "There's not much time between them. Even if we decided to pass up on Goldie and go and look at this other horse now, we might miss Juniper as well if we don't hurry back."

Issie shook her head. "It doesn't matter, Tom. I don't care if we miss the whole auction. You have to come and see this grey pony. He's the one. I know it sounds stupid and all that and I can't explain it, but he is. You have to come and meet him!"

"Issie." Avery didn't move. "It's easy to fall in love with a pony, but really you need be sensible here.

If we don't bid on Goldie and the grey pony doesn't turn out to be right for you then you may not get a horse today at all." He didn't need to add the next half of that sentence because Issie knew what he meant: *This is your last chance*, he was telling her, *your last chance to buy a pony and make it to pony camp.*

Issie looked at the auction ring. She could bid on Goldie now and forget about the grey pony. That would make sense, wouldn't it? Goldie was wonderful after all; there was nothing wrong with her.

But the grey pony was different, he was special. Issie knew at that moment that she couldn't just forget about him. It was a risk she had to take – she had no choice.

"Come on," she said to Avery. "Follow me. You're going to love him. His name is Mystic…"

If Avery did love Mystic then he made a good job of hiding it. "His conformation is sound enough," he said. "Good legs and hooves, but look at that sway back!"

"Is that bad?" Issie asked.

Avery shook his head. "Well, it doesn't mean you

can't ride him. A horse with a sway back can still be quite sound and healthy, but it is a sign of old age." He opened Mystic's mouth and peered hard at his teeth.

"At a guess, I'd say this pony is even older than eighteen. He might be as much as twenty-five, which is very old indeed in horse years."

"Does that mean you won't let me buy him?" Issie braced herself for bad news.

"I didn't say that," Avery reassured her. "He seems to be fit enough, and as long as his paces are still OK and he's not stiff in his joints I have no problem with his age." He turned to Issie. "What do you say? Want to take him for a test ride?"

The man who had nearly run Issie over helped them to saddle Mystic up. "He comes with all his own tack," he told them. "Saddle, bridle and a summer rug and winter rug."

"Who are his current owners?" asked Avery.

"The girl already asked me that," the man replied. "Sorry, but I can't tell you. I'm just here to sell on their behalf. You know as much about this pony as I do."

Issie was nervous as she climbed the mounting block and put her foot in the stirrup. "Do you think he's safe to ride?" she asked Tom.

Avery nodded. "He has a kind face – I don't think this pony's got a nasty bone in his body. And look at the way his ears are pricked forward," he said. "That means he's happy." Avery gave the grey pony a pat. "No, I get a good feeling about this gelding. I think he's a trustworthy soul."

Avery was right. From the moment Issie sat in the saddle on this pony, she knew she could put all her faith in him. Mystic didn't put a hoof out of place. His ears swivelled back and forth as he listened to Issie's cues, and his paces were so precise, it was almost as if he knew what she was thinking and was anticipating her next move, reacting before she asked him to. His walk was loose and free and his trot had a pep to it that belied his age.

"Try asking him to canter now," Avery instructed.

The moment Mystic rose up into a canter, Issie's face broke into a broad grin. "He feels like a rocking horse!" she laughed. "It's so comfy!"

Avery nodded. "He has three excellent paces, no stiffness and a solid temperament."

Issie pulled Mystic back up to a trot and brought the grey pony over to Avery. "Does that mean we can buy him?"

"If that's what you really want," Avery said. He looked at his watch. "But you need to make your mind up now. Juniper is due to go in the ring at any minute. Do you still want to bid on him as well? If you do, we'll need to hurry back."

Issie shook her head. "No, Tom. I'm sure. I want to buy Mystic."

"OK," said Avery, "it's your decision. But Mystic is old and you don't want to be buying trouble. At his age, I think it would be wise to get a vet check done first before we bid." He turned to the man who was selling Mystic. "Is that OK with you?"

"Fine by me, mate," the man shugged. "Like I said, it's not my horse, so I don't care whether you buy him or not. But aren't you cutting it a bit fine for time? The vet's trailer is at the far end of the field. You can book him in, but you'll have to be fast if you want to get it done before the auction. This pony is due in the ring very soon." The man stepped back inside the horse truck and left Issie and Avery alone to talk about what to do next.

"Tom!" Issie whispered to her instructor. "Maybe he's right. We don't have enough time..."

Avery shook his head. "There's enough time.

Mystic is lot 99. I'd say that gives us about an hour to get the job done." He checked to make sure the man wasn't listening to them and then whispered, "If you ask me, this guy is just trying to put us off getting the vet check. Owners will always discourage a vet check, but I think it's worth doing one."

"OK," Issie nodded, "let's do it."

"We're going to go ahead with the vet check," Avery informed the man.

The man nodded. "Righto, but if you haven't come back to me in time, I'm taking him into the ring. He has to be sold today."

Avery turned to Issie. "Go and get your mum. She and I will sort out the vet. You can wait by the auction ring and keep an eye on the horses. Let us know if we're cutting it too fine."

"OK!" Issie said. She left Avery with Mystic and ran back through the barn, searching the stands for her mum.

"Where have you been?" Mrs Brown wanted to know.

Issie explained how she had found the grey pony at the last minute. "Avery needs you to come and help him," Issie said. "He's organising a vet check."

"A vet check?" Mrs Brown was confused. "But I

thought you were buying the palomino or the bay?"

"I've changed my mind," said Issie. "Mum, hurry, you need to go now; there's not much time."

There was even less time than Issie thought. She watched as two more horses entered the ring and were sold quickly. Then it was Juniper's turn. The little bay fetched $900, which was well within Issie's price range. Issie felt a pang of regret as she watched the bidders battle it out for the bay pony. Juniper could have been hers today. Was she wrong to let him go? Issie felt better about losing him when she saw that the winning bidder was a girl about her own age. Her father made the bid for her and the girl was smiling from ear to ear as the auctioneer's gavel fell. "Sold to the girl in the blue shirt – happy riding!" the auctioneer said.

Two more horses came into the ring after that. Issie wondered if Avery and her mum had managed to organise the vet check yet. *Never mind*, she thought. Mystic was lot number 99. They still had plenty of time.

"Number 65 is scratched," the auctioneer called. "Can we have lot number 66 into the arena please?" The auction ring remained empty and then the auctioneer called again. "Lot 66, can we have you in the arena now please! Lot 66!"

As lot 66 finally entered through the barn doors Issie felt the blood freeze in her veins. "Here we are! Lot 66," the auctioneer called. "A grey pony, eighteen years old, fourteen hands high – a one-in-a-million learner's pony!" Issie couldn't believe it. Lot 66 was Mystic!

But it couldn't be! This was all wrong. Mystic wasn't 66. He was… number 99! She looked at the number on the grey pony's rump. It said 66! But it hadn't before: it had said 99, she was sure of it… And then she realised what had gone wrong.

Of course! The man at the blue truck must have stuck the number on upside down by mistake! She would have realised his mistake if she'd seen the number on Mystic's registration, but the paper had been crushed under the pony's hay net.

No wonder the man had told Avery there wasn't enough time for a vet check. He wasn't trying to put him off after all. He just didn't realise he'd stuck the sticker on upside down! He must have only noticed the mistake just before entering the ring, because the sticker was now the right way round, but it was stuck on clumsily with the glue peeling away, like it had been hastily ripped off and plonked back on again.

Mystic was now being led around the ring and the

auctioneer was beginning his chant. "How much am I bid for this little grey pony here? Like I said, this pony is a one-in-a-million learner's mount, worth his weight in gold no doubt. Eighteen years young, ladies and gents, every inch of him is fit and sound… and we're going to start the bidding at $200. Will anyone offer me $200?"

Issie didn't know what to do. She didn't have a clue how to bid by herself. She wasn't even registered. She would have to wait and hope that her mum and Avery came back soon.

"Who'll give me 200? Do I have 200?" The auctioneer was calling faster and faster now, trying to stir up a bid from the crowd. "100!" he shouted. "Do I have $100?"

Still there was silence. *Maybe no one will bid,* Issie thought hopefully, *then we can buy him privately after the auction is over.*

In the ring, Mystic's head was held high as he looked around at the crowd. Issie could have sworn that the grey gelding had picked her out from all the faces surrounding him and held her gaze, looking at her as if to say, *Why aren't you buying me? What's wrong?*

"Who'll give me $100? Do I have 100, 100?" The

auctioneer's patter was getting him nowhere. No one was going to bid on this old, swaybacked grey pony. Mystic was about to be passed in with no bids.

"Come on, people. I have instructions to sell this pony today!" the auctioneer shouted. "Who'll give me 100?"

"Fifty!" There was a shout from the crowd and the auctioneer's chant suddenly changed.

"I have $50; the bid is now with the gentleman over there!"

Issie turned round to see where the bid had come from. She felt as if someone had just punched her in the stomach and knocked all the air right out of her. It was Nigel Christie!

"I have $50, $50. Who'll raise it to 100?" the auctioneer shouted.

Issie felt her palms sweating, her head spinning. The knacker's yard man had just bid on her pony! She looked frantically at the door to the barn. Where were her mum and Avery? They needed to make a bid now!

"I have $50, going once, going twice..." The auctioneer was winding up and still there was no sign of either Avery or her mum. Issie realised she had no choice: she was going to have to make a bid herself.

"Going once, going twice, going three times..."

"$100!" Issie squeaked out, raising her hand. But the auctioneer hadn't seen or heard her and he brought the gavel down hard with a bang.

"Sold to Nigel Christie!" he shouted. "Can we have the next lot, number 67, into the ring please?"

And with that, Nigel Christie led Mystic back out of the arena, leaving Issie trembling with shock. Her special pony, her Mystic, was gone.

# CHAPTER 10
### *The Worst Christmas Ever*

When Mrs Brown saw Issie running towards her, tears streaming down her cheeks, she didn't understand what was wrong.

"Don't worry. We've found him," she told Issie. "We've booked the vet and he can do it straight away."

"No!" Issie managed to gasp. She was trying to get her breath back, struggling to stop crying. "No, Mum! It's too late."

"Sweetie – he's not in the ring for a while yet. I'm sure we'll have time…"

"The number," Issie panted, "the number on the rump was upside down and I didn't look at the papers properly – Mystic was number 66 not 99!" She saw the realisation dawn on her mother's face. It was already too late. They had missed the auction.

"Issie!" She looked up to see Avery striding towards her, accompanied by a sandy-haired man in green overalls carrying a satchel.

"Issie, this is Mr Adams," Avery said. "He'll be doing the vet check for us today."

"No," said Issie, "he won't be. Tom, we got the auction number wrong. Mystic has already been sold – to Nigel Christie."

It took a moment for everyone to grasp the situation. Then, once apologies were made to the vet, Avery, Issie and Mrs Brown headed at speed for the battered green horse truck where the man who sold Mystic was packing up to go home.

"The grey pony? Yeah, he's gone with Christie already," he told them. "Sorry you missed out. I really didn't think you guys were serious bidders to be honest. I thought the vet check was just an excuse and you were looking for a way to wriggle out of it."

"Is Christie still here?" Avery asked. "The auction is only halfway through; he must still be buying."

"I don't think so." The man shook his head. "He said he'd bought six horses already – that's a full truck load. I think he's gone."

It looked like the man was right. There was no sign of Christie or his truck anywhere on the grounds. Still Issie didn't give up on Mystic. She spent an hour walking pointlessly up and down the aisles of horse trucks and floats, checking all the pens in case he was still there somewhere. Finally, she had to admit defeat. Christie was gone and the little dapple-grey had gone with him.

The auction, meanwhile, was still in full swing. "They're up to lot 103 now," Mrs Brown pointed out to Avery and Issie. "There are still a few ponies to come. Is it worth checking to see if there's anything else to bid on?"

Issie knew what her mum was trying to do. She was desperately trying to fix things, to make it all better. She was trying to save Issie from the awfulness of driving home with that empty horse float, knowing that she had lost Mystic forever. But it was too late for that now and Issie knew it.

"It's OK, Mum." Issie shook her head. She didn't care about the auction. As far as she was concerned, it was over. "I just want to go home."

The next day at school, Stella and Kate were horrified when Issie told them what happened at the auction. She didn't tell them about her dream though. How could she explain that she knew this pony was destined to be hers? That before they even met she somehow had a mystical connection with the grey horse. Issie still didn't understand it herself.

"You should have bid on the palomino at the start!" Stella said. "I love palominos." This sort of advice clearly wasn't helping. Issie had already spent the whole of the night before lying in bed, thinking about everything she did wrong and how she would do it all so differently if only she had the chance to reverse time. She was still certain she had done the right thing by deciding to buy Mystic instead of Goldie or Juniper. She just wished the auctioneer had heard her bid. "I shouted out $100," she told the girls, "but he didn't hear me!"

"They should hold the auction again; they made a mistake. Why didn't you tell them they got it wrong?" Stella said. "You made the top bid!"

"I did tell them!" Issie groaned. "Mum went and told the auctioneer, but Nigel Christie had already given them a cheque and left with the horses. Also,

I wasn't even supposed to be bidding anyway. I wasn't registered and I'm only a kid; Mum was supposed to bid for me. They said they couldn't do anything about it, that once the hammer came down and the horse was sold, that was it!"

"So what are you going to do now?" asked Kate.

"I've been trying to track Christie down," Issie said, "but he's moved. Nobody seems to know where his farm is now. Tom is still looking for him."

"Ohhh!" said Stella excitedly. "If you find him then we should mount up on Coco and Toby and do a midnight raid on his farm. We could herd up all the horses he has and take them home with us so they'll be free!"

"Yeah, Stella, that's a really good plan," Kate said sarcastically. "Has anyone else got a suggestion that isn't ridiculous?"

"Can we not talk about this any more?" Issie pleaded. She knew Stella and Kate were just trying to cheer her up, but she didn't want to talk about imaginary rescue missions. She couldn't even bear to think about the fact that Christie had Mystic. He would keep him grazing at the yard, but then sooner or later… Oh! It was just too awful! She mustn't think about it! How could she have let Christie take him? To find her perfect pony and then to lose him again was just too cruel.

That night Issie fell into a fitful sleep. Her dreams flickered like candles in the darkness, and when she woke up she couldn't remember them exactly. But she remembered certain feelings and images. She remembered the grey pony galloping towards her out of the blackness, his mane trailing out like silver flames. There was a moment when her eyes met with those of the little grey, and in that instant she knew he hadn't left her. She knew in her heart that Mystic was still alive.

Was the dream real? Issie had to hope so. After all, her first dream had led her to the grey pony. She had to believe that there was still a chance.

Avery was still looking for Christie but there was no news. For the rest of the week Issie moved through the world as if she wasn't really there. It was the last week of term, and the rest of Miss Willis's class were all in high spirits at the prospect of the upcoming holidays. There was no more homework and even the lessons were fun, since most of them involved making Christmas cards or decorations. Issie tried to get into the Christmas spirit. But she had never felt more miserable.

Each day Issie went through the motions, trying to pretend her life was still the same. She got dressed, went to school, sat down for dinner each night and pushed her food around on the plate, to at least make it look like she was eating so that her mum wouldn't worry. But inside, she was hollow with grief. It was like there was a piece of her missing and she didn't know how to find it and put herself back together again.

Issie had felt this way before she realised. It was a bit like when she had to say goodbye to Bert. It had been awful enough saying goodbye to the strawberry roan pony. But with Mystic? It was like losing Bert times a million.

At least Bert had been going to a good home, Issie thought with a shiver. There would be no happy ending for Mystic. Even worse, she could have saved him. It was all her fault. Maybe she had been dreaming all along and it was time to face the truth. She had lost her horse forever, and there was nothing she could do about it.

The best thing about being totally miserable on Christmas Eve is that you can watch loads of bad television. There is nothing quite like drowning your sorrows with rubbish TV if you're trying to escape from the awfulness of your actual life.

So on Christmas Eve at three in the afternoon Issie was still in her pyjamas lying on the sofa watching *The Muppets' Christmas Carol* when there was a knock at the front door.

"Can you get it, Mum?" Issie said, not moving from the sofa.

At this moment, most mums would have told their daughter to stop being a princess and get off the sofa and answer the door. But Mrs Brown knew Issie too well. She could tell that her daughter wasn't just being a drama queen, and she was really worried about her.

Over the past week since the auction Mrs Brown had tried several of her patented cheer-up chats. She'd been resolutely upbeat as she told Issie that there were other ponies out there, even better ones than Mystic, and it was only a matter of time before they found her one.

When the pep talks failed, though, Mrs Brown knew her daughter well enough to sense there was something deeply wrong. Ever since the auction Issie had retreated inside her shell like a hermit crab and nothing her mother did – and she had tried every trick in the book – was getting through to her.

And so, when the doorbell rang, despite the fact that she was up to her elbows in Christmas trifle preparations, Amanda Brown didn't bark at her daughter to get up and answer it. Instead, she put down the bowl of custard and whipped cream and went to the door herself. She wasn't at all surprised to have a Christmas Eve visitor. In fact, she had been expecting him...

"Tom! So glad you could come!" Mrs Brown said as she swung the front door open.

"Merry Christmas, Mrs B," Avery said, smiling. Then he added enigmatically, "I've got brilliant news about...

about that thing we were discussing on the phone…"

"What thing?" Issie popped her head up over the sofa.

Avery looked at Mrs Brown. Issie could have sworn something weird was going on between them. She saw the pair of them share a conspiratorial smile. Then they both looked back at her blankly.

"It's nothing," said Mrs Brown. "Nothing you need to worry about. Tom and I were just arranging what he was going to bring tomorrow. I've invited him over for Christmas morning and then he can come with us to the beach to meet up with Stella and Kate for lunch."

"Oh," Issie said. She was a little surprised by this news. Her mum had never mentioned before now that they'd be having guests. She thought it would just be the two of them this year.

"Is this a good time to talk?" Avery said. "I can always come back later…"

"No, no, please stay!" insisted Mrs Brown. "Come in and talk to me while I mix the trifle cream." She cast a glance over at Issie who had sunk back down on to the sofa. "Issie, why don't you go upstairs and get changed? You can't lie around in your pyjamas for the entire day."

Actually, Issie didn't see why she couldn't do just that if she wanted to. But she did as her mum said. By the time she came back downstairs, her mum had finished making the trifle and she and Avery had obviously had their chat because he was saying his goodbyes and heading for the front door.

"Issie," said Avery, "I really have to get going, but before I do, I wanted to ask you something."

Issie knew her mum would have told Avery everything, about how miserable she'd been since losing Mystic at the auction, and how even the thought of Christmas couldn't cheer her up. She figured she was in for one of Avery's pep talks now, and she wanted to point out to him that her mum had already tried that and it hadn't worked. How could she explain to Tom that she was too heartbroken over Mystic to talk about it any more? That she instinctively knew he was meant to be her pony and that she had let him down terribly.

She needn't have worried, though, because as it turned out, Avery didn't appear to be interested in cheering her up after all. "I just wanted to ask…" Avery paused, "…erm… what size are you?"

"What do you mean?"

"I mean what size clothes do you take? Are you a small? Medium? I'm not very good at guessing these things – I suppose I should have just asked your mum. I hope it's not embarrassing to..."

"It's fine," Issie said flatly, then she added, "I'm a medium."

"Excellent!" said Avery. He looked at his watch. "Well, I have some things to do. I'd better be off. See you tomorrow in time for present-opening!"

And with that, Avery left. Issie was stunned. She had always thought Tom Avery was just like her, that he felt as passionately about horses as she did. Surely he must have understood how unbearably awful it had been watching the grey pony being taken away by Christie. But if he did, he certainly wasn't showing it. Her instructor was bright and breezy and acting as if the disaster at the auction had never happened.

"Why did you ask him round for Christmas?" Issie grumbled to her mum over dinner that night.

"Tom is new to town, Issie. He hasn't had time to make many friends yet and he doesn't have any family here," said Mrs Brown. "Besides, I thought you'd like it if he came over. I know this has been a tough week.

I figured it would cheer you up to have someone else here."

A tough week? *Tough?* It had been the worst week ever! Issie couldn't believe that her mum and Avery didn't get what she was going through. She sank deeper into depression and deeper into the sofa, and spent the rest of Christmas Eve back in her pyjamas watching even more rubbish TV. Normally on the night before Christmas she stayed up as late as she could, trying to make it until midnight so that it would officially be Christmas Day and she could open her presents. But even that prospect didn't hold its usual thrill this year. The week's events had drained her emotional batteries.

"I'm going to bed," she told her mum finally at nine o'clock.

"Really?" Mrs Brown was puzzled. "But it's so early."

"I know," Issie said. "I'm just really tired."

"OK," her mum smiled. Issie was about to walk out of the door when she added, "Sweetie, I know that this Christmas hasn't been what you were hoping for, but you have to have a little faith, OK?"

*Faith?* Issie couldn't believe it. At this rate, her mum would be telling her to ask Santa for a pony!

*This is definitely the worst Christmas ever,* Issie thought as she lay on her bed. She stared at the walls around her. They were covered from floor to ceiling with pictures of ponies. Most young girls had posters of pop bands on their walls, but Issie had spent years collecting copies of *PONY Magazine* and pulling out the posters, plastering her wall with horses of all shapes, sizes and colours. Her favourite picture was the one just above her bed end. It was a grey pony cantering through a field of bright red poppies. The pony in the picture looked a bit like Mystic, Issie thought. A dapple-grey with coal-black eyes and a flowing mane and tail.

She wondered where Mystic was right now. Then a shiver ran down her spine as she imagined the worst. Issie wished she could have saved him. She wished Mystic could have been her horse.

"If he was mine," Issie said out loud, "I would love him so much, he would be my horse forever, and he would love me too and stay with me and never, ever leave me."

Some kids believe in magic at Christmas time, but Issie Brown was not one of them. As she turned over in bed that Christmas Eve and switched out her light, she felt like the whole Christmas thing was over for her. She was ten, after all, and maybe that meant Christmas had lost the power to surprise her.

She couldn't have been more wrong.

# CHAPTER 11
### *The Christmas Present*

Issie's family had always opened their presents the moment they woke up on Christmas Day, a tradition that made both Stella and Kate extremely jealous.

"My mum makes us all wait until my cousins arrive before we open ours," Stella had grumbled when Issie told her this.

"Ohmygod! My house is even worse!" Kate complained. "We have to eat lunch first!"

Well, that wasn't how they did Christmas at Issie's house. The rule was that you opened your presents as soon as you got up. And so, when Issie woke at 7 a.m., still feeling kind of Grinchy, she decided the best thing to do was to put on a brave face, try and cheer up and kick the day off by unwrapping a few presents.

"Actually," Mrs Brown said when Issie came into the kitchen, "we're not doing the presents yet."

Issie's face fell. "What?"

"Since it's just you and me this year, I thought it would be more fun to wait until the others get here," said Mrs Brown.

"What others?"

"Tom is due before lunch." Mrs Brown paused. "And I've asked Stella and Kate to pop over here, so we need to wait for them too."

Issie was surprised by this. "You asked Stella and Kate? Aren't we just going to meet them down at the beach like we normally do?"

"I thought you'd be pleased that your friends are coming over," said Mrs Brown.

"I am, but…"

"Good! They're due at ten. You can watch TV until they get here while I finish my mince pies."

More bad Christmas TV! Issie turned on the telly. There was another Muppet special. And several movies featuring Santa. She settled on *Miracle on 34th Street*, which she hadn't seen before, and lay on the sofa while her mother clattered around in the kitchen. The film was almost finished by the time Avery turned up. He was holding two presents, one under each arm, and for the first time since Issie had met him, he was wearing ordinary clothes instead of his usual cheesecutter cap, boots and jodhpurs.

"Merry Christmas!" he said, passing Issie her present. Issie took the package and gave it a squeeze. It was soft and quite light. Her first present of the day! She was about to open it when Avery suddenly reached out a hand and snatched it back from her.

"On second thoughts," he added, "you can't have this yet. I'll give it to you later."

It was bad enough having to wait to open your presents – but now they were being taken back again! Issie was totally bemused by this, but she didn't have the chance to ask Avery what was going on because at that moment Stella and Kate arrived.

"Ohmygod! I don't believe it! Issie! Isn't this exciting?" Stella squealed. Avery and Mrs Brown both froze and Avery shot her a look that made Stella immediately shut up. "Ummm… I mean it's so exciting all of us being here and opening our Christmas gifts together. That's all I was saying," Stella added, looking uncomfortable.

"Wow!" Issie looked at Kate. "Is everyone going to act super-weird today?"

"There's nothing weird going on," Kate said, looking nervous. "What do you mean weird? It's not like we've all got a big secret or anything. We're all just here to open our presents, OK?" Issie wished she had never said anything. Kate was acting even nuttier than Stella.

"Right, everyone into the living room!" Mrs Brown led the way with a big plate of Chrismas mince pies and fudge to snack on and they all settled around the tree ready to hand out the presents.

"Here's one for you, Kate, and one for you, Stella." Mrs Brown passed a gift to each girl. "And for you, Tom, and Issie!"

It didn't take them long to work their way through the pile under the tree. Most of the girls' presents, as always, were pony-related. Issie had bought a fancy hoof-pick for Kate and a book for Stella about horse breeds of the world, which the girls pored over, picking out the ones they liked best. As usual, Issie had been stuck for something to buy her mum and in the end she had got her a bottle of perfume, which Mrs Brown seemed pleased with. The two boxes from Issie's dad turned out to be exactly what she had expected: a board game (Monopoly) and a make-your-own jewellery kit.

"I'll call him later to say thanks," Issie told her mum. It still felt weird not having her dad here, but her mother was right – present-opening was better this year with lots of other people around.

There were still a few gifts left. "We can open them later," said Mrs Brown. "Right now, I think it's time for you to open your main present, Issie."

Issie looked under the tree. "No, it's not under the tree," Mrs Brown said. Then she pulled something out of her pocket. It looked like a long black scarf.

"Is that my gift?" Issie was puzzled.

"No," said Mrs Brown. "It's a blindfold. You've got to put it on before we lead you to your present." Issie looked at Stella and Kate who were both grinning from ear to ear.

"Do you know what it is?" Issie asked them.

"Uh-huh," Kate nodded, "but we promised your mum we wouldn't tell."

Issie felt her heart racing. So that was why Stella and Kate had been acting so strangely! They knew about the secret present – whatever it was.

"OK," Issie said, reaching out to take the blindfold, "I'll put it on."

"No, you won't!" said Stella. "You could cheat. Let your mum do it so we know that it's on properly and you can't see."

Issie stood up and her mum wrapped the black scarf around her eyes, securing it tightly with a knot at the back of Issie's head.

"Can you see?" asked Kate.

"No," Issie said. It was a weird feeling: everything was pitch-black and although she couldn't see anyone, she could feel their eyes on her.

"Let's spin her round!" Stella said. Issie felt Stella and Kate's hands turning her, and heard the girls giggling as they span Issie round and round.

"Are you dizzy yet?" asked Mrs Brown.

"We are!" Kate laughed.

"I think I'm going to fall over!" Issie shrieked.

"OK, that'll do. Lead her through," said Mrs Brown.

By now the blindfold had slipped just a bit. Issie could see a tiny bit out of the gap at the bottom, just enough to glimpse her feet and figure out where she was going, as Stella and Kate led her through the living room and out into the back yard.

"Look out, there's a step coming up," Kate cautioned her as she led Issie across the paved courtyard and on to the back lawn.

Then Issie heard Avery's voice ahead of her. He must have been in the back yard on the lawn waiting for them. "Are you ready?" Mrs Brown asked him.

"Yep," Avery answered. "You can take off her blindfold now."

Issie's heart was pounding in her ears. What was so amazing that everyone else was in on the surprise and she needed to be blindfolded and escorted outside to see it?

Could it be what she thought it was? Issie had given up hope of a pony, but maybe she had given up too soon? She was so excited she just wanted to rip off the blindfold. Instead, she took a deep breath, trying to stay calm as her mum untied the knot.

"It won't come undone!" Mrs Brown said.

"Mu-uum!" Issie squeaked. She was so excited now she could hardly stand it.

"Wait a minute." Mrs Brown's fingers fumbled with the knot. "Wait a minute. I've got it… there!"

The blindfold fell away and Issie blinked as her eyes adjusted to the light. Everything was blurry at first. She could make out the shapes of Avery, Stella, Kate, her mother. And then next to them, on the lawn, another shape. She blinked and looked again.

It was a bike.

A bike. A brand-new, bright blue bicycle, tied up with a big bow on the handlebars. "Surprise!" said Mrs Brown.

Issie was so crushed she couldn't believe it. In that instant, she knew she had been utterly stupid to expect Mystic to be there waiting on the back lawn for her. She was an idiot. And yet she couldn't help how she felt now, the bitter sense of disbelief as she stood there, unable to speak, staring at her new blue bike.

"Do you like it?" asked Mrs Brown.

Issie didn't know what to say. She felt sick inside. She should never have got her hopes up like that! What was she thinking? For a brief moment, when that blindfold had been put on and Stella and Kate had spun her round and led her outside, Issie had managed to convince herself that her pony would be waiting for her. Now, as she looked at her mother's kind, expectant face, she knew she had to be a good actress and pretend to love the bike. She couldn't be ungrateful and ruin the surprise that her mum had planned so carefully for her. There was nothing else for it. She had to lie.

"It's great, Mum." Issie managed a smile. "Thank you so much."

"Are you sure?" asked Mrs Brown expectantly. "Because if you don't like the colour, we can always swap it. I was worried that you might not like the colour."

"The colour is great, honestly. Blue is my favourite colour." Issie's fake, cheery smile was beginning to slip, but she was determined not to let her mum know how heartsick she was feeling right now.

Standing next to her, Stella and Kate began to giggle. Her mum was grinning too. Issie's smile faded totally now. She didn't understand why her Christmas present was so funny to everyone.

"Come on, Amanda," Avery said to Mrs Brown. "I think it's time you put Issie out of her misery. You need to tell her exactly why you've bought her the bike."

Issie was confused. What did Avery mean by that? "Mum? What's going on?"

Mrs Brown put her arms round Issie. "This bike isn't just a gift for you," she said.

"It's not?" Issie was even more confused.

"It's a gift for me too," Mrs Brown said. "You

know how I hate being a taxi service," she continued. "This seemed like the best solution. I won't have to drive you. You can ride your bike down to the River Paddock every day."

Issie still didn't get it. "Why will I be going down to the River Paddock?"

Mrs Brown looked at her daughter. "Isadora! If you own a pony, you've got to feed it and check on it every day. I thought you knew that."

"But I don't own a pony!"

Her mother smiled. "Yes, you do."

"What?" Issie couldn't believe it. "Mum? You bought me a pony?"

"Not just any pony," said her mother. "The grey pony from the auction, the one you wanted so much."

"Mystic? Mum, you bought Mystic!" Issie was completely overwhelmed. "But how? I saw Christie take him…"

"It was all Tom's doing," said Mrs Brown. "He finally managed to track Christie down and suggested a private deal to buy the pony back."

"Let's just say I made a late bid," said Avery, smiling.

"We didn't want to tell you about it in case we didn't pull it off," Mrs Brown continued. "It took ages just to hunt down Christie. When Tom came around yesterday he told me that he'd finally found him and made an offer."

Avery nodded. "In the nick of time as it turned out. I gave Christie cash on the spot for Mystic and he accepted the deal straightaway. He let me take the pony home there and then."

"Ohmygod!" Stella said. "I can't believe we all managed to keep this a secret from you. Your mum told us all about it yesterday and asked if we wanted to come over and see your face when she told you."

"I'm sorry you were so miserable yesterday, sweetie," Mrs Brown added, "but we didn't want to tell you about Mystic until I was sure I could buy him back. And then, by the time Tom had the good news it was already Christmas Eve. We thought, why not wait one more day and it would make a great Christmas surprise…"

Issie was still stunned. "So Mystic's really mine? For real? For good?"

"Uh-huh," Mrs Brown smiled. "He's really yours."

"Come on," Avery said. "You can try out your bike another time. What say we all drive down to the River Paddock and see your new pony?"

It was in the car on the way to the paddock that Avery finally handed over Issie's present. "I was about to give it to you before," he explained, "and then I realised it would give the game away."

Issie took the squishy-soft gold-wrapped package for a second time, and this time Avery didn't snatch it back. She dug her fingers into the gold wrapping paper and ripped it open. Inside, she felt the soft rasp of wool against her fingers. She closed her hands around a navy blue wool knitted jersey and pulled it out of the gold paper.

"There should be something else in there too," Avery said. Issie dug around in the gold paper and pulled out a red tie.

"It's your new club uniform," said Stella.

"You'll need it if you're going to come away with us on camp," Kate added.

"Welcome to the Chevalier Point Pony Club," Avery said. He pulled the Range Rover up at the paddock gate and turned to her. "We'll wait here. You go and catch your horse."

Issie couldn't actually see Mystic in the paddock. There were Toby and Coco, grazing together as usual by the river's edge. It took her a couple of moments to scan the field and find the third horse. He was facing away from Issie and his dapple-grey rump was all she could make out at first. Then, at the sound of the car door slamming, the grey pony raised his head and looked around.

Issie felt her heart skip a beat when she saw his face. It was really him! "Mystic!" she called out. The dapple-grey saw her too and nickered a greeting. "Mystic!" Issie instantly broke into a run, sprinting across the paddock towards her pony.

"Hey! You forgot your halter!" Stella yelled after her. "Issie? How are you going to catch him?"

Issie didn't care – she was in such a mad panic to reach her pony. When she was a few metres away from the grey gelding she finally stopped running. This paddock, the other horses, it was all new to Mystic. If she charged up to him, she might spook him.

Issie needn't have worried. Mystic seemed quite

happy with his new home. The little grey walked straight up to her until he stood in front of her, his snowy face not more than a metre away as he fixed her with a level stare from those gentle, coal-black eyes.

"Hey, boy," Issie said, smiling back at him. "I didn't think I was ever going to see you again." She reached into her coat pocket and produced a carrot, extending her arm to offer it to her pony.

Mystic took a step towards her and stretched out his neck to reach the carrot, using his velvety soft lips to snuffle it up out of her open palm. "It's OK." Issie's voice was choked with emotion as she spoke to him. "You're home now, Mystic. I'm so sorry. It was all my fault. I'll never lose you again, I promise."

Her hands were trembling as she reached out to stroke the pony's neck. She ran her fingers through the coarse ropey fibres of his mane, feeling the smooth sleekness of his dapple coat underneath. And then, before she could stop herself or worry any more about spooking him, she had flung both her arms around Mystic's neck. She hugged him, hanging on tight, her face buried in Mystic's silvery mane, inhaling his sweet pony smell. It was the best smell in the world, and the best feeling she'd ever had in her life.

Issie could have stayed like that forever. But there were people waiting for her. She looked up and saw Stella and Kate looking on impatiently. Her friends had never met Mystic before. They wanted to finally say hello to the little grey pony that had caused all this fuss.

Issie gave the girls a wave. "We're coming!" she called.

She didn't have a halter to lead her horse back, but it didn't matter. She just kept one hand wrapped in Mystic's mane and the little grey seemed to understand that she wanted him to follow, falling into step beside her as they walked back together across the paddock.

"Come on, boy," she murmured to her pony. "They're all waiting for you. It's time to show them how special you really are."

# CHAPTER 12
### *Forever*

Years later, Issie still remembered that Christmas as the best one she ever had. The moment when she had been reunited with her pony was kept locked in her heart forever. Whenever she felt sad or lonely or nothing seemed to be going right, she thought about what Avery and her mum and her friends had done for her that Christmas. Mystic's arrival had turned out to be more significant than any of her friends could ever know. *It's funny*, Issie thought now, *how a single event can turn your life around so that nothing will ever be the same again.*

"Remember that day?" Kate laughed, chopping up the last of her apples. "It was so cool the way you totally lost it when you saw him in the paddock for the first time."

"Yeah," agreed Stella, "but the best bit was in the garden at your house when you thought the bike was your real present and you were trying to be nice and not hurt your mum's feelings! Honestly, Issie, you should have seen the look on your face!"

"You thought that was the best bit?" Issie was boggled by Stella's sense of humour sometimes.

"I'm sorry, sweetie," Mrs Brown said. "I know I shouldn't have done that to you. But Stella's right – it was hilarious. You tried so hard not to look heartbroken when we took off the blindfold and you saw that bicycle!"

"Yeah, well," Issie grinned, "it turned out OK in the end. I'm still using that bike; it was a good present."

The best present, though, had been Mystic. Two days after Christmas, Issie had saddled up her new pony and, along with Stella and Kate and the rest of the Chevalier Point Pony Club, she had set off to pony camp.

Trekking out was the perfect way to get to know her new horse. Issie had been a little nervous as they set off across the open fields. Would Mystic be well-behaved or would he get worked up and spook or shy at every shadow like some horses do? Issie should have known better than to worry. Mystic was the most bombpoof and well-mannered pony on the trek. He loved being out in the open countryside and as she rode him carefully and considerately, with her hands always light against the bit and her voice always calm and gentle, the bond between pony and rider grew even stronger.

When they returned from pony camp, Mystic and Issie fell into a blissful routine. Each day she would cycle down to the River Paddock to check on her pony. In summer she would ride him out on hacks with Stella and Kate, or sometimes she would ride out alone down the road to Avery's farm where she would meet her instructor for lessons in the arena.

In winter, even when it was too wet to ride, Issie would bike down to the River Paddock every day to make sure that Mystic's cover was on straight and to check that he was dry and warm. Sometimes, if it was very chilly and there was frost on the ground, she would mix up warm mash into Mystic's hard feed. Then she would watch the pony as he snuffled down his food, giggling at the plumes of warm, steamy breath coming out of his nostrils whenever he lifted his head out of the bucket.

Mystic's dapple-grey coat had grown shaggy under his rugs during the winter months, so when spring finally came and he began to shed his winter coat, little tufts of grey hair were left lying everywhere from the curry comb she used to groom him.

As for Issie, the changes in her over the months weren't so obvious, but they were just as real. Now that she finally had her dream pony she was determined to be the best rider that she could be. She learnt fast under Avery's tuition, mastering her first pony club D certificate with ease. As her skills grew, so did the bond between her and Mystic. Their understanding of each other became stronger every day. Issie had compiled a mental list of all her pony's silly quirks: how he loved carrots but wasn't fussed about peppermints; how he loved to be groomed in that sweet spot just behind his ears; how sensitive he was when you did up his girth and liked it to be eased up slowly.

Horses are not angels of course. It is not unusual to have a pony that bites or kicks, bucks or shies. In fact, some will do all four things at once! But not Mystic. He didn't have a mean or naughty bone in his swaybacked body. He was the perfect pony, there was no doubt about it, and Issie loved him absolutely and completely.

And then, a year after Mystic came to the River Paddock, Issie lost him again. If that Christmas Day when Mystic arrived had been the best day of her life, the day at pony club when he was killed had to be the worst.

Issie's mum and her friends knew how devastating Mystic's death was for her. They felt her pain, and they didn't want to hurt her more, and so, as time passed by, they seldom, if ever, mentioned his name. But in the kitchen on Christmas Eve it seemed right somehow to talk about him, to remember the little grey pony that meant so much to her.

"Mystic was really special, wasn't he?" Stella said as they stood together. "He used to make me laugh – the way he would always whinny out to Coco if they were in separate paddocks."

"He was a really good jumper," said Kate. "It was like he didn't realise how old he was. Mystic thought he was still a colt."

Issie giggled at this. It was true; she had never thought of the grey gelding as being old – even though he was.

"I know it sounds ridiculous," Mrs Brown said to her daughter, looking serious now as she wrapped an arm around Issie's shoulder, "but I do believe he knew what he was doing when he saved you that day at pony club. I saw that accident happen and it was the strangest thing, the way he reared up to face that truck and threw you backwards so that you were clear. I had never seen Mystic rear in his life, but it was as if he was trying to get you out of the way, like he wanted to protect you."

She hugged her daughter tight. "I really do think he did it for you, Isadora." She smiled. "Sometimes I feel like he's still here with you. Do you know what I mean? I know that sounds crazy, but…"

"No, Mum," Issie said, choking back her tears. "It doesn't sound crazy at all…"

If only her mum and Stella and Kate knew about the very special bond Issie still shared with Mystic.

When Issie had promised her pony that she would never lose him again, she had meant it. *Forever*, she had said. She remembered that. And so did Mystic. Death hadn't been the end of her bond with the grey pony. He was still hers somehow – and she still belonged to him. Whenever she needed his help, Mystic was there for her, like a guardian angel. Not a ghost, but a real horse, always by her side. He would never leave her and she knew that. She had faith in him.

Mrs Brown gave Issie a squeeze and then released her from her hug. She looked around the kitchen. "Would it be too much to ask for my kitchen back?" she smiled at the girls. "I need to make the pudding for tomorrow and I don't want to get chaff and alfalfa in it by mistake."

"It's OK, Mrs B," Stella grinned. "We're nearly done. We just have to pack the mixture into the ice-cream tubs."

Five tubs were set up along the bench, each one had slices of carrot and apple laid in a pattern at the bottom. "It's like a jelly mould," Kate explained to Mrs Brown. "When we turn the cake tins upside down the carrots and apples will be on top as decoration."

"Why are there five cakes?" Mrs Brown wanted to know. "Don't you only need four?"

"Ummm – I made an extra one," Issie said.

"Greedy Blaze!" Stella giggled. Issie didn't say anything.

It took the girls another half an hour to finish the cakes. When they were done and the kitchen was cleaned, they let the cakes set while they watched a Christmas movie. It took a long time for Issie, Stella and Kate to say goodbye. There was much hugging and cries of Merry Christmas, despite the fact that they would all be seeing each other the next day for Christmas lunch on the beach. Eventually, Kate's mum, who had arrived to take Stella and Kate home, got tired of waiting and leant on the car horn to hurry them up. Issie waved goodbye to her friends, waiting until they drove out of sight. Then she lifted her three ice-cream containers into the basket on the front handlebars of her blue bike and set off towards Winterflood Farm.

It was getting late by the time she arrived there, almost dinner time, but there was still at least an hour of daylight left. The days were so long at this time of the year, it wouldn't get properly dark until eight.

The sound of the bike tyres on the gravel driveway alerted Avery to Issie's arrival and he was at the front door waiting for her by the time she had parked the bike.

"Christmas Cake? For me? You shouldn't have!" he grinned.

"I didn't!" Issie grinned back. "You know they're for the ponies."

"Well, actually, I've got some Christmas cake already. I baked it myself," Avery said. "Why don't you come in and have a slice after you've fed the ponies? I'll put the kettle on. Blaze and Nightstorm are both out the back in the magnolia paddock and I've told them that you're bringing presents."

Issie nodded. "See you inside in a minute then!" She picked the three cakes up out of the basket and headed past the rows of neat, green hedging and post and rail fencing, around the side of the house towards the paddocks. Avery was right. Blaze and Storm had been expecting her. They both had their heads over the fence waiting for her and Issie marvelled at the similarities between mother and son.

Storm was getting bigger every day. The colt was only a few months old, but his legs were so long it was clear already that he would grow bigger than his mother. His conformation had the same stocky, powerful build as his father, the great stallion Marius. His face, though, had the beauty and finesse of his dam's Arabian bloodlines. Their colouring was different – Blaze was chestnut while Storm was a deep russet bay – but both mother and son shared the same striking marking, a broad white blaze.

"Hey, you two," Issie said. "I've got Christmas cakes for you."

Blaze and Storm might not have known what a Christmas cake was, but they knew hard feed when they saw it. Issie upended the ice-cream tubs into their feed bins and was pleased that the feed stayed in a perfect mould shape and did actually look a bit like Christmas cake. She smiled at the sight of her perfect creations, and then laughed out loud as both Storm and Blaze shoved their muzzles into the feed bins and bit into their Christmas gifts, instantly mushing it up.

Issie stood there for a moment watching her horses eat. And then she took the third ice-cream tub and upended that one too, into another feed bin which she set down alongside the two horses.

Would he come for it? Would he be here today? Issie didn't know. Mystic usually only turned up if there was trouble afoot, at a time when she desperately needed him. And she didn't need him today, not really. But it was Christmas. A time when you should be with the ones you love. Even if Mystic couldn't be here with them, she wanted him to know that he was in her heart. She hoped her horse knew that even when he wasn't here, he was never, ever forgotten.

"Merry Christmas, Mystic," said Issie. She stood in the paddock with tears in her eyes, waiting and hoping. The light was fading now and it was getting dark. For a moment longer she stood there. Then she gave Blaze and Storm a pat and walked inside the house where Avery was waiting for her with tea.

At the back door, she paused for a moment to shuck off her boots, but she didn't turn around. If she had turned at that moment, she would have seen that there was a third horse in the paddock with Blaze and Storm. A little grey gelding, about fourteen hands high, his dapples faded and his back swayed with age.

All Issie needed to do was look back over her shoulder and she would have seen the grey pony standing there, eating his Christmas treat alongside Blaze and her foal. But Issie didn't look back. She didn't need to. She knew he was there.

# Pony A to Z

Are you a totally horsey girl? Check out this glossary of horsey words and see how many you already know!

**AIDS** – the signals a rider uses to let their horse know what she wants him to do. There are two kinds of aids – natural and artificial. Natural aids include using the seat, legs and hands. Artifical aids include using whips, spurs, martingales and nosebands.

**ARENA** – also known as a school or manege, the arena is a purpose-built area, usually made from sawdust or sand, where you can ride and train your horse.

**BAY** – a reddish-brown coloured horse with black points and black mane and tail.

**BIT** – made of metal with rings on either side to connect it to the bridle. The bit goes into the horse's mouth and the rider uses it to guide and control their horse. There are lots of different kinds of bits. One of the most common bits is a snaffle.

**BRIDLE** – this fits on the horse's head. The reins are attached to it, which the rider holds to guide and control the horse.

**CANTER** – faster than a walk or a trot, the canter is a three-beat pace.

**CAVESSON** – a type of noseband worn on the horse's bridle.

**CAVALETTI** – low jumps constructed from a single bar that is nailed to two crossed poles at each corner. Cavaletti are only little jumps but they can be stacked up to make bigger fences or used for gridwork.

**CHESTNUT** – a chestnut horse is ginger or reddish in colour with a matching mane and tail.

**COLT** – a young male horse.

**DUN** – dun-coloured horses vary from mouse to golden, and generally have black or chocolate points and a black or chocolate mane and tail.

**DUNG** – horse poo!

**EARS** – you can tell whether the horse is happy or not by its ears. Horses will put their ears flat back against their head when they are angry or frightened.

**ELIMINATED** – if a rider has three refusals on a showjumping or cross-country course they will be eliminated or disqualified.

**FARRIER** – once known as the "blacksmith", the farrier is the person who puts metal shoes on your horse. Horses need to be shod at least every six weeks.

**FILLY** – a young female horse.

**FLANK** – a very sensitive area of the horse located on their side, just in front of the hind leg.

**FLAXEN** – some chestnut horses have a flaxen mane and tail, meaning they are pale blonde in colour.

**FOAL** – a baby horse.

**GALLOP** – the fastest of the horse's four paces. When a horse gallops it lifts all four feet off the ground at once.

**GELDING** – a male horse that has been gelded is like a cat that has been neutered.

**GIRTH** – the thick piece of leather that goes around the horse's belly to hold the saddle in place.

**GREY** – a grey horse has both white and black hairs throughout its coat. There are different kinds of grey: a dapple-grey has circular blooms of grey, especially on the rump; a fleabitten grey has tufts of dark hair, a bit like freckles.

**HALTER** – the halter is worn around the horse's head and allows the rider to control the horse while they are on the ground – tying up the horse for grooming, feeding etc.

**HANDS HIGH** – the height of a horse or pony is measured in hands. One hand equals four inches. Measurement is made from the ground next to the hoof up to the wither. A pony is any animal that measures up to 14.2 hands high. A horse is any animal larger than 14.2.

**HOCK** – the area halfway up the back of a horse's hind leg, where a point (hock) sticks out.

**IMPULSION** – the push or energy a horse uses to move forward powerfully. This is a term that dressage riders often use.

**IN FOAL** – when a mare is "in foal" it means she is pregnant and is going to have a baby.

**JODHPURS** – stretchy, snug-fitting trousers worn by horse riders. Also known as "jods", they should be cream or white for competitions.

**JUMPING** – horses love to jump! However there are some reasons why they might stop jumping or refuse, including being overfaced with fences that are too big and loss of nerve on the rider's part.

**KIT** – your grooming kit should include: a dandy brush, a body brush, a hoof pick, a curry comb, a sweat scraper, a mane comb and a sponge.

**LAME** – lameness means that a horse is sore in one or more of its legs. Some causes of lameness are stone bruises, a pricked foot from a misplaced nail during shoeing and laminitis (fever in the feet).

**LEAD ROPE** – this attaches to the halter and is used to lead and tie up the horse or pony.

**LIVER CHESTNUT** – a liver chestnut describes a particular colour of chesnut horse that is darker and more chocolate-toned than a regular chestnut horse or pony.

**LOOSE BOX** – a large indoor space big enough for a pony or horse to move around and lie down, with a floor lined with straw, shavings, sawdust or some other non-edible, comfortable bedding material.

**MANE** – the long hair that runs along a horse's neck. The mane needs to be brushed and combed regularly and can be pulled or plaited.

**MARE** – a female horse.

**MOUNT** – another word for your horse. Getting on the horse is referred to as "mounting" and you can use a "mounting block" to climb on to your horse.

**NEAR** – the left-hand side of a horse.

**NOSEBAND** – there are different kinds of noseband including a cavesson and a flash. Nosebands attach to the bridle and are artificial aids used to control the horse.

**NOVICE** – a new, less-experienced rider.

**NUMNAH** – a pad, shaped like a saddle, that is worn underneath the saddle to protect and cushion the horse's back and to stop the saddle getting sweaty.

**OXER** – a strong fence consisting of railings. Oxers can be jumped on the cross-country course or in showjumping.

**PACES** – horses and ponies have four paces: walk, trot, canter and gallop.

**PADDOCK** – also known as a field, this is an outdoor space where the horse is free to roam and graze on grass.

**PIEBALD** – a black and white coloured horse with large, irregular patches, a bit like a magpie.

**POLL** – a very sensitive area between the horse's ears on the top of their head.

**PLAITS** – when a horse or pony goes to a show or event they will often wear their manes and tails plaited.

**QUARTER HORSE** – the Quarter Horse is a special breed, often favoured by riders in Western films, known for its intelligence and strength. Quarter Horses are often "cowboy colours" such as Palomino, Dun and Piebald (also known as Tobiano).

**R**

**REINS** – these attach to the bit and are held in the rider's hands to control the horse.

**REFUSAL** – when a horse stops and will not jump it is called a refusal.

**RUG** – horses who live outside in paddocks or fields will require a paddock rug or cover to keep them warm and dry, especially in winter.

**SADDLE** – usually made out of leather, the saddle fits on to the horse's back and makes it more secure and comfortable for the rider. You can get different types of saddles to suit different activities, like jumping, dressage and cross-country.

**SKEWBALD** – a coloured horse with irregular patches of white and any other colour except plain black.

**STABLE** – an indoor space where horses and ponies are kept warm and dry. In New Zealand horses are seldom stabled and tend to live out at pasture, but stables are still used sometimes especially on very cold or wet nights.

**STALLION** – a male horse that has not been gelded. Stallions are considered to be more difficult to manage than mares and geldings.

**STIRRUP IRON** – the metal stirrup or stirrup iron, attached to the saddle, is where the rider puts their foot while riding. It should be big enough for the rider to allow half an inch on each side of their foot.

**TACK** – this is a horsey term for saddlery: all the bits and pieces you need to ride, like bridles, saddles etc. When you get a horse ready to ride you are "tacking up".

**TOBIANO** – similar to piebald and skewbald, a term particularly used for American breeds such as the Quarter Horse.

**TROT** – there are two ways of riding the trot. You can do a sitting trot where you stay in the saddle, or you can do a rising trot where you allow the horse's stride to lift you up and down out of the saddle (this is also known as posting).

**UNSADDLE** – taking the horse's tack off, including the saddle and bridle.

**VET** – the vet should be called in to treat a horse that is unwell or injured.

**VICES** – bad habits such as bucking, rearing, kicking and biting.

**WALK** – the slowest of all the horse's paces.

**WITHER** – the wither is at the base of the neck, where the saddle sits. It is the point on the horse's body where their height is measured.

**WHITE** – there is actually no such thing as a "white" horse; they are known as "greys".

**EXERCISE** – horses need to be exercised regularly with lots of trotting and canter work to get them fit if they are competing.

**YEARLING** – a horse or pony which can be either a boy or girl, under one year of age. Yearlings are too young to be ridden.

**ZEBRA** – zebras are related to horses. Like horses, zebras can walk, trot, canter and gallop, but they cannot be trained or ridden.

# Don't miss

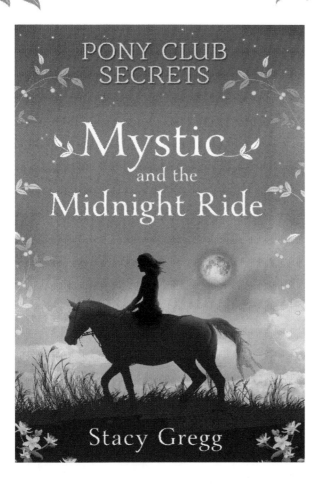

PONY CLUB
SECRETS

Mystic
and the
Midnight Ride

Stacy Gregg

Issie loves horses more than anything! And she especially
loves her pony Mystic at Chevalier Point Pony Club. So
when the unthinkable happens, Issie is devastated.
Then her instructor asks her to care for Blaze, an
abandoned pony, and Issie's riding skills are really put
to the test. Will she tame the spirited new horse, Blaze?
And can Mystic somehow return to help her…?

PONY CLUB
SECRETS

Blaze
and the
Dark Rider

Stacy Gregg

Issie is riding for Chevalier Point Pony Club at the
Interclub Shield – the biggest competition of the year!

But disaster strikes when equipment is sabotaged and one
of the riders is injured. Issie needs Mystic's help again…

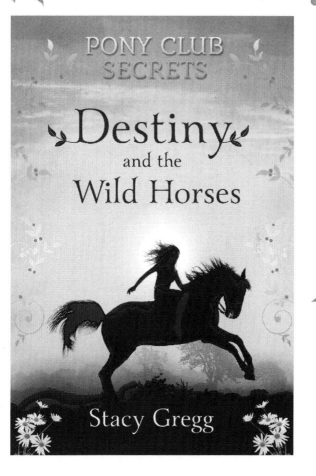

PONY CLUB
SECRETS

Destiny
and the
Wild Horses

Stacy Gregg

Issie and her horse, Blaze, are spending summer at her
aunt's farm instead of at pony club. When Issie hears of
plans to cull a group of wild ponies she's determined to
save them. This time, Issie is going to need
all the help she can get...

Every girl dreams of becoming a princess.
But this real-life princess has a dream of her own.

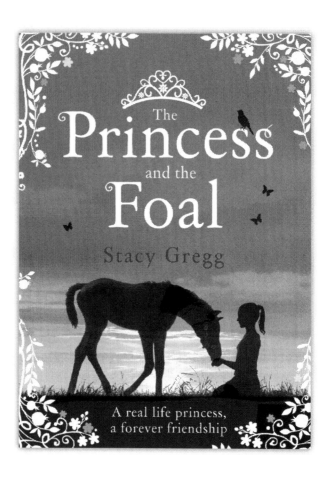

Discover the incredible story
of Princess Haya and her foal.

OUT NOW